TRUTH &
REVENGE

SHEILA RAWLINGS

For Martin

ACKNOWLEDGMENTS

My greatest thanks go to my husband Martin, whose continued help and encouragement during the writing of this book kept me focussed.

I would also like to thank Tommy Leighton for the time, effort and advice he gave me in reading and editing my first novel.

CHAPTER 1

Monteriggioni, Italy 1986: Betrayal

Roberto was desperate. His last hope dashed, he knew it was only a matter of time before they came looking for him.

His heart was beating fast as he hurried back to his car and an overwhelming sense of panic was starting to creep through his body.

He had to get back to his family before the inevitable happened.

The hot Italian sun blazed overhead and it was difficult for him to determine whether the beads of sweat on his forehead were induced by heat or fear. He mopped his brow, scrunching his handkerchief tightly before stuffing it back into his pocket.

He replayed in his mind the meeting he had just left with a man he had thought was his friend. Their families had known each other since the war and the two boys had played together in the school holidays. He thought he knew him, but today he had seen a man he did not recognise. He felt betrayed.

He climbed into his car and sat for a while, hands gripping the steering wheel while he tried to think of a last way out of his treacherous situation. But nothing came to him. So he started the car and began the short journey back home to his wife who had also been so sure that their friend would help them. It pained him to destroy her faith in friendship.

As Roberto pulled up outside the humble dwelling that he and his family shared, the door was flung open and his wife came running out to meet him, with their six-month-old baby in her arms. The child, perhaps sensing its mother's anguish, was crying inconsolably. He tried to appear brave for their sakes, but he knew that it was a futile gesture.

"What did he say," she asked, before he had time to get out of the car, gently caressing her baby in an attempt to calm the distraught infant. "Can he get the money to you in time? You told him how urgent it was, didn't you Roberto?"

Roberto got out of the car and stood staring at the ground, unable to look his wife in the eyes.

"He said he isn't in a position to help," he lied, knowing that the answer had been more forceful than that – a point-blank refusal. "He said he can't lay his hands on that kind of money at such short notice. I'm sure he would, if it were possible." His wife was not fooled. She knew her husband too well. She realised she was covering up for the man who was obviously not the friend he had pretended to be, and who had now condemned them to their fate.

"May he rot in hell," she cursed, her eyes almost black with fury. Roberto put his arm around her and stroked his child's face with his free hand. The panic he had felt earlier for their safety was becoming harder to control. Time was running out, though, so he began to hurry her towards the house.

"Isabella, I must get you and the children away from here," he said sharply. "We don't have much time. They will be here by nightfall and I don't want you anywhere near the house... or me. It's me they're after, and I don't want to risk them using my family as leverage. I'll take you to your parents' house. You should all be safe there. I'll come back here and try to buy some more time."

Standing her ground, Isabella looked deep into her husband's eyes and released herself from his grip. "I am not leaving you on your own to face those *parassiti*," she hissed. "I am your wife and we will face them together. Even they would not hurt a woman with young children. I am not afraid of them, only for you *caro*."

Her blazing eyes filled with tears and as Roberto gently wiped them away, an intense feeling of pride for his wife welled up inside him. Fully aware of the danger he had selfishly put them in, she would stand by him and now he just wanted to protect the thing he valued most – his family. Isabella was still as beautiful as the day he married her, and the fierce strength she now displayed in defence of those she loved only served to make him feel just how unworthy he was of her devotion.

He had always met her pleas to stop gambling away money they did not have with assurances that it was only a few games of cards with friends. What he had failed to admit was that his gambling had become an addiction. Now, after getting himself involved in a high-stakes game run by a local gangster, he found himself in debt to the tune of 23 million lira, with no possible means of paying it back.

Today was collection day.

"Isabella," he whispered gently. "I can't put you or the children in danger for my stupidity and weakness. Please, let me take you to your parents and I promise you I will take care of the situation. He replaced his arm around her waist and, before she could protest again, pulled her through the door of the house, where a wide-eyed, five-year-old boy was waiting for them.

Roberto let go of Isabella and gently closed the front door, then took the boy's out-stretched hand. He crouched down beside him, pulling him into his arms and holding him tightly.

"You are going to have to be the man of the family now, little one," he said to his son, trying not to display any signs of emotion. "You must look after your *mamma* and sister for me until I can be with you all again. You must be good for your grandparents and do what ever they say without complaining. I will come for you as soon as I can. Remember, you are Italian and Italian men are brave."

The boy threw his arms around his father's neck and Roberto felt his heart break. How could he put his family through this pain?

Gently pulling his son's arms free, he stood up and was about to utter a few more words of comfort when the sound of a car crunching on the gravel as it pulled up outside the house made him start. They were early!

Signalling to his wife to be quiet and take the children into the lounge, he furtively peeked through the hall window and saw three burly men getting out of the black Mercedes-Benz sedan. Despite the fact that all three wore dark glasses, he recognised them as the heavies that had been present at the game and felt his heart pounding. They did not look in the mood to negotiate.

"De Luca," the biggest of the trio shouted, throwing his burnt-out cigarette onto the ground and treading it into the gravel. "The boss wants his money, so you'd better come out and pay up or we'll come in and show you the consequences of reneging on a deal."

Roberto leant with his back against the door, trying to figure out his next move. They could make a dash for it out of the back door, but his car was out front and they would never make it to safety on foot – not with two small children in tow. He knew calling the police would be futile, as the men's boss was in cahoots with the chief of police. There was nothing else for it, he had to confront them and hope he could stall for time. At least he could divert their attention away from his family.

Looking at Isabella, who had returned to the hallway, he took her face in his hands and kissed her. She threw her arms around his neck.

"Please don't go out there," she cried desperately. "They will kill you. There must be someone we can call."

Roberto carefully released himself and tried to give her a reassuring smile.

"There's no one," he said. "I have to face them. Otherwise, they will come inside. We must think of the children. Go to them and keep them safe. I love you *cara*. Always remember that." Isabella fought back the tears and, kissing Roberto softly on his lips, went back to the lounge. Roberto sighed, took a deep breath and opened the door.

The men watched him walk slowly out of the house and descend the few short steps. Time seemed to stand still momentarily as they eyed each other up and down, the men waiting to see how Roberto would react. Roberto was first to break the tension.

"I need more time to get Signor Rizzo's money. It's a lot to get hold of. I need to call in a few favours but I can assure Signor Rizzo that he will be repaid in full." He hoped they had not noticed the sweat now cascading down his forehead.

The gang's self-appointed spokesman, a man in his late thirties with rough stubble on his chin and a thick gold chain, visible beneath his open-necked shirt, walked towards Roberto, stopping a few feet away from him.

"Signor Rizzo wants his money *now*," he said menacingly. "He's already given you longer than agreed. He's not a patient man. Are you going to pay or not?"

Roberto took another deep breath and silently prayed to God for strength. "I don't have the money now," he repeated. "I really need more time."

The man glanced back at his two companions and, walking towards Roberto, sighed. "Then we will have to show you what happens to people who disappoint Signor Rizzo, my friend."

Roberto did not see the first punch coming. He felt a searing pain in his stomach as he doubled up and sank to the ground. The first blow was followed by another stronger punch to his face, breaking his nose and leaving him writhing in agony. Before he had time to defend himself, all three heavies had joined in the assault and were relentlessly kicking every part of his body as he lay crying out in pain.

Isabella could not stop herself. She rushed out of the house to find her husband unconscious and bleeding profusely into the gravel. The men stood over him as she rushed to his side, screaming his name. Anger took hold of her as she beat her fists hard on the first man's chest.

Without flinching, he grabbed hold of her wrists and pulled her towards him, glaring into her terrified eyes.

"This is what happens to people who don't honour their debts," he hissed in her face, turning and spitting onto the lifeless body of Roberto. "Just think yourself lucky that my father is a gentleman who respects women. I myself do not, but fortunately for you I respect *his* wishes. As you can't repay the debt, my father wishes to inform you that your house and property is now forfeit to him. You have two days to pack up and leave. You won't get another warning. Next time we will come and take what is now rightfully ours, whether you are here or not!"

He pushed her roughly to the ground, turned and, followed by the other two, got back into the car and drove off, leaving Isabella to crawl over to Roberto and cradle him in her arms. The tears were now rolling freely down her cheeks and dripping onto her husband's face.

"Roberto," she cried, kissing and stroking his forehead and trying to rouse him. "*Caro*, please speak to me. I'll get help. Just open your eyes and look at me." She kissed his lips and taking a handkerchief from her pocket, tried to wipe away some of the blood. Roberto groaned and gradually opened one eye, the other being too swollen and bloody to respond.

"I'm sorry," he rasped, coughing blood out of his mouth. "Please forgive me. I've let you and the children down but I love you, *cara*.

Please. Never forget that." He tried to raise his hand to her face but it never made it. As it fell back to the ground with a dull thud Isabella felt his body go limp.

"Roberto," she screamed, patting the side of his face and trying to shake life into his listless body. His lifeless, single open eye stared unblinkingly up at her. He was no longer in pain.

Isabella threw herself across his body and cried uncontrollably. Her whole world had begun to crumble around her and she wanted to die with her husband. Through the tears, she was aware of a small voice calling to her from the doorway.

"Mamma, why is papa lying on the ground? He'll get all dirty." Her son was looking at her, innocently waiting for an answer. She knew her grief would have to wait. She had to be strong and protect her children, but the anger raged inside her.

They would pay for this. They would *all* pay."

CHAPTER 2

Poggibonsi, Italy 2006: Revenge

It was New Year's Day 2006 and Santo Rizzo was working late in his office. His wife had taken umbrage over a rather enthusiastic kiss he had enjoyed with the host's wife as they saw in the New Year at a friend's house.

A heated argument had ensued on returning to their own home, so he was in no hurry to repeat the experience, her mood being no less antagonistic when he had left earlier that morning.

They had married young, when he had still been working in his father's café-bar in Capaci, Sicily. She was a popular local beauty and he had prided himself on being the one to successfully win her affections from amidst her throng of young admirers. As his fortunes steadily began to rise – largely as a result of his growing involvement with influential, if dubious, businessmen he had been introduced to by friends – she had proved an excellent asset. A beautiful woman on his arm had made him the envy of all the men at many a social occasion, and Santo loved attention and power.

However, the acquisition of such beauty had come at a price and, after moving to Tuscany, he soon discovered that beauty was not his wife's only weapon. She also possessed a passion for shopping and the high life, as well as an extremely spiteful tongue, all of which overshadowed her slow wit. In short, she was costing him a fortune and providing him with a constant headache. Their rows had steadily increased until the point that it was now difficult for him to spend any length of time with her, except at formal or social occasions, where the presence of others meant he could leave her in the hands of other unfortunate listeners.

The two sons that she had borne him were also slow-witted, but their hefty size had proved useful in handling situations that required brawn rather than brains. His lucrative, albeit illegal, gambling and money lending activities had more than made use of their particular talents. They at least knew how to discreetly deal with troublemakers without drawing attention to him. He was well respected by some of Tuscany's most high-powered figures and preferred not to have his position of power compromised by inconsequential nobodies.

It had long since grown dark outside and, because it was a national holiday and he was alone, he had only switched on his desk lamp. He preferred the soft, comforting light it emitted to the harsh glare that came from the fluorescent light of the main office. He had unplugged his direct telephone line and switched off his mobile, in order to get some peace from his wife. In the past, just being in the office had proved an inadequate barrier to her nagging; better not to take any chances.

Santo finished signing the letters his secretary had left on his desk the day before and lent back in his chair, closing his eyes to enjoy the serenity that enveloped him. He would probably look in at his club on the way home and enjoy a brandy or two, to numb the effects of the lecture he knew was coming upon his return home. He could not even count on his sons to distract her, as they had both wanted to spend time at home with their wives and children this year, eschewing the family get together he usually hosted. He would, therefore, have to face her alone. He sighed at the thought.

He opened his eyes, logged out of his computer, drained his now lukewarm cup of coffee and put on his coat. Switching off his desk lamp, he slowly made his way towards the door, which was illuminated solely by the dim light from the corridor. Making sure that the office door was securely locked behind him, he left the building, nodding to the security guard on his way out, walked around the back of the office block and down an alleyway towards the deserted car park. His car stood all by itself in its usual reserved bay, lit by a solitary lamppost.

As he put his key in the lock of the car door, he felt an arm wind vice like around his neck and the cold steel of a gun pressed against his temple. The catch of the gun clicked back, and the sensation of warm breath passed over his ear.

"*Buona sera, Signor Rizzo*," hissed his unseen assailant. "I've been waiting for you. It's taken me a while to get you on your own, but I'm a very patient man. We have some unfinished business to attend to, my friend. Rest assured, I will also be paying a visit to those Neanderthal sons of yours, but I thought it only right for you to be the first.

"Roberto de Luca sends his apologies but, due to the disrespectful treatment he received from your gorillas, he is unable to come himself. However, allow me to present his calling card."

With that, he spun Santo round, threw him back against his car and pulled the trigger of his gun. The bullet hit Santo directly in the forehead and with a look of shock still etched on his face, he slid down the side of the car.

As he landed in a heap on the ground, terrified eyes still staring into space, his killer spat on his lifeless body.

"Don't worry," the man hissed. "You will have plenty of company in hell. I'm saving the biggest betrayer until last."

The shot had reverberated back up the alleyway towards the office block. The startled security guard took his gun from its holster and sprinted out of the building to investigate.

He was too late. Santo was dead and there was no one else to be seen.

CHAPTER 3

London, summer 2012: Opportunity

"Oh hell!" thought Chris as she glanced at the clock and jumped out of bed. "I'm going to be late again. Feldman is going to kill me!"

She hurriedly dressed, gulped down a rather strong cup of coffee, then made a grab for her coat and rushed out of her flat, slamming the door behind her.

It was at times like these that she cursed living on the third floor. When her father had first decided to invest in a flat in London, so that she did not have to waste her money renting, it had seemed a good idea to be above street level and away from traffic noise. However, when it came to rushing down six flights of stairs whenever she was in a hurry – which had become a frequent occurrence – the idea seemed to lose some of its appeal. She was sure that one day she would trip up in her haste, arriving at the bottom faster than anticipated.

Having worked hard to obtain a degree in marketing and media studies from Edinburgh University, Chris had finally managed to get a marketing job with Feldman & Son. As an international company there was huge potential for her to do well. There was also the added bonus that her new boss was extremely good looking. All the ingredients were there for her to excel, if she could just learn to get out of bed earlier!

Out in the busy street it felt as if people were conspiring against her desperate attempt to reach the office on time. Groups of elderly women appeared in her path, gathered in leisurely conversation in the summer sunshine; a never-ending stream of cars came from nowhere as she tried to cross the road, and inevitably the tube was both delayed and crammed full, forcing her to wait for several trains to pass before she managed to squeeze into one. This usually happened when she was in a hurry, and why was there always someone immediately in front of her who had a problem with their Oyster card at the barrier or a tourist struggling to understand the intricacies of the ticket system?

On arrival at the office of Feldman & Son, a smart building in the heart of Mayfair, she smiled at the male receptionist while flashing her pass at him. Tim Meyers had only been with the company a few months but had made it his business to recognise all the members of staff who worked there. He was a tall, well-built lad with auburn hair and freckles. Although only twenty-one, he was confident and self-assured, and flashed Chris a cheeky grin while glancing briefly at the clock. "Morning Miss Newman. I think Mr Feldman has beaten you to it today."

That boy is far too cheeky, she thought as she rushed to the lift. As the doors opened at the first floor, she dashed up the corridor towards her office, the sound of her footsteps reverberating loudly. "Damn these wooden floors!" she cursed.

As she swept through the open plan area, she was aware of playful banter being exchanged by some of the marketing team who occupied it. "Must be time for coffee, here comes Chrissie," and "I didn't know she worked part-time now!" It was like a broken record to Chris, who had received this greeting every day so far this week. However, they were the least of her problems, she still had Feldman to face. With a bit of luck he may not have noticed her absence. He was usually too involved with the day's work schedule to notice her, even when she was there. She opened her office door gently, hoping to slide behind her desk and assume a relaxed pose, in order to give the impression of having been there for a while.

Unfortunately for her, Simon Feldman had chosen that day to talk to her about expanding their client base and was impatiently pacing the room, inspecting his watch intermittently.

"Miss Newman!" he exclaimed sarcastically, spotting her through the glass partition as she strode into her room. "How good of you to drop in and see us this morning."

Chris smiled apologetically, knowing that whatever she said would not prevent the forthcoming lecture.

"Are you trying to create some sort of record, Miss Newman? This is the third time you've been late this week and it's only Wednesday! Is there any chance of receiving a full day's work from you sometime or shall I arrange for a temporary replacement until you can see your way clear to giving us your undivided attention?"

He was looking at her intently with his head slightly on one side and one of his eyebrows raised, waiting for a reply. He was only four years older than Chris, but his detached manner made him seem much older.

"I'm really very sorry Mr Feldman," Chris managed to say, while her boss paused for breath. "It really won't happen again, I promise you. I just don't seem to be able to hear my alarm clock these days. I must be becoming immune to it."

She gave him a sheepish smile.

Simon Feldman looked at her impatiently. This girl really was the limit. She had no idea of punctuality and her desk always looked like a battleground. Despite this, however, she was showing signs of becoming a damn good assistant.

The fact that she was also quite attractive had not been lost on him either. Those baby blue eyes, long, soft, fair hair and cute smile were too much for any man to reprimand for long, even a serious man like Simon.

Two years ago, when he had taken over the family business, following his father's retirement due to ill health, he had not relished the idea. He had taken a gap year after university to travel around Europe, particularly Italy, where his late grandmother had been born. Having been spoilt as an only child and indulged as an adult, he had not given much thought to matters of responsibility. Joining the company had allowed him to enjoy many benefits without the inconvenience of having to earn them, unlike many of his contemporaries. However, he had a tendency to be introverted and found it difficult to deal with the new authoritative role he had been thrust into.

His father's illness had rather thrown him into the limelight, in which he felt uneasy, especially when it meant being responsible for other people. However, having spent a good deal of his working life continuing to build up the business that Simon's grandfather had started, his father had been keen to keep the family tradition going and wanted his son to be the one to take it forward.

As a result he had now become quite an earnest young man, believing that the only way to assert authority was to be aloof and formal. The arrival of Chris had at least added a bit of light relief to the job. She was very easy on the eye and pleasant to work with and did not demand too much of him.

"Perhaps we should club together and rent Big Ben for you in future," he snapped half-heartedly, accepting the fact that he was not going to be able to keep up the 'angry boss man' act for much longer. "In the meantime," he continued, " I have an assignment for you."

Chris sighed with relief at the mention of work. At least he was not going to fire her today. She threw off her coat, which landed half on and half off her chair, grabbed her notebook and pen and followed her boss into his office where he motioned her to sit down.

"I've been reviewing our list of clients," he said opening a file on his computer, "and I've decided that it's time we attracted some new ones. As you know, we already have quite a few foreign clients who have accounts with us to market their products over here, but we've never seriously tackled the home market. This is a pretty competitive area, so we need to be sure that we have a solid strategy and a presentation to highlight our strengths and the level of service we can offer when approaching prospective new clients."

He looked up at Chris momentarily to observe her reaction before continuing. He had found since working with her that her face always betrayed her true feelings. It was therefore almost impossible for her to hide her enthusiasm or disapproval of things. By the way she was hanging on to his every word he knew that, this time, he had her full attention.

"I've drawn up a list of companies I think we should contact," he continued, "in order to persuade them that we could find a better market for their merchandise abroad than any of our competitors. The names of the people you need to speak to are also listed."

He handed her a sheet of paper with eight names on it. Chris read the list carefully. They were mostly unknown to her, although she vaguely recognised one of them.

"I had the research boys working overtime to come up with possible candidates," he said, watching her digest the list, "and out of the twenty-odd names they came up with I chose those eight. I think they should prove to have the most potential." He took back the sheet of paper and glanced at it for a while, then took up his pen and put a tick against four of them.

Handing the sheet back to Chris, he said: "I'm going to give you responsibility for handling those four and I'll take care of the remaining ones. Get the art department to update our current PowerPoint presentation, with special emphasis on testimonials from satisfied clients for us to show these people. They're already working on our new promotional material, so they should have all the current data readily to hand. We'll need to get it burned onto half a dozen

CDs so that we can leave copies with them. We ought to have a few hard copy presentation folders too, so that we cover all options."

"When do you want me to start making phone calls?" asked Chris. He had never asked her to do anything like this on her own before and she felt a nervous flutter in her stomach, although the challenge and the opportunity to prove her ability was very appealing.

"As soon as possible," he replied. "These people are all new to selling their goods abroad and I don't want anyone beating us to the punch, so make sure those bods in the art department get a move on. They'll sit on it for weeks if you don't hustle them. But before you start contacting anyone, I'll just run over a few guidelines to help you with the initial approach."

Over the next half an hour, Simon outlined the best way of introducing the company to potential clients, stressing that the principal objective was to obtain a face-to-face meeting. Chris listened attentively, asking questions and making notes. Now that he had demonstrated confidence in her, she was eager to make a start on the task. When she was satisfied she had understood all of his instructions, she thanked him for his advice and went back to her office.

He watched her go out and smiled to himself. She had only been working for him for six months, but having accompanied him to various meetings and liaised with several of the company's suppliers, Simon felt she had demonstrated the necessary skills and diplomacy to deal with existing and potential clients directly. He had every faith in her.

CHAPTER 4

Chris decided she would need some down time after work to recharge her batteries for the task ahead. She was determined to get as many meetings lined up as possible and felt sure that she would be able to follow through with some positive results. However, despite her optimism she could not stop a few annoying self doubts creeping into her mind.

After her meeting with Simon, she spent a good part of the morning talking to the art department about the updated PowerPoint presentation, including the CDs and hard copies that he had requested. As usual, it proved to be an unpleasant experience.

The art department was made up of three designers. Brad Martinez, an American of Puerto Rican descent on his father's side; Sue Taylor, not long out of art college but with a head full of self importance, and Pete Bradshaw, a nerdy young man who took care of the company's website. Each one of them thought that the inner sanctum of the art department was a place of reverence and that the rest of the company should bow to their combined genius.

"When did you say you want all this?" Brad asked arrogantly. As the senior member of the department, he enjoyed making the most of his status.

"Tomorrow morning would be good," Chris replied, trying not to show how much the design team made her nervous. Why did they have to be so aggressive and argumentative?

"We've already got Feldman breathing down our necks for the new promotional material," he snapped, "and Pete has been working overtime on the redesign of the website. Creativity requires time you know. We really should have more time on this. Can't you use the old stuff for now?"

Sue looked up from her screen at Brad, quietly smirking, before shifting her gaze to Chris to judge the effect of Brad's words. She turned away and winked at Pete, who had also been trying to stifle a smirk.

Chris took a deep breath and moved slightly closer to Brad, looking him squarely in the eyes.

"This is important," she stressed. "We need to start contacting people as soon as possible, before we miss the boat with their business. Mr Feldman is already trying to set up a meeting for tomorrow, so it's vital that we have everything ready to make a professional pitch. Anyway, the old stuff is out of date."

She felt a surge of annoyance, which gave her the confidence to push the point home.

"This may very well be the first time that any of these potential clients have heard of us. First impressions are everything. I don't want to risk us looking anything other than a professional organisation. *You*, supposedly, are the professionals – so get cracking please!" She glared defiantly at Brad, who sniffed and fleetingly glanced at the other two, both of whom had returned their attentions to their screens.

"OK, leave it with us," he uttered begrudgingly. "We'll take a look at it this afternoon."

Chris breathed a secret sigh of relief.

"Fine," she replied. "When it's been approved I'll need copies on six CDs, as well as two hard copies. If you could email me a copy of the presentation when it's done that would be great. I will then check it and get Mr Feldman to sign it off, so that you can finalise the package."

With that she turned and left the department, unaware of the mocking gestures from the three designers behind her.

* * * * * * *

Having spent the remaining part of the day doing some research, Chris found herself sitting in Toppers, the local wine bar, at six-thirty with a half empty glass of white wine in front of her, waiting for her friend Tessa to appear. She and Tessa had been at university together doing the same marketing course. They had instantly hit it off and had stayed firm friends since graduating. Whenever she felt anxious or under pressure, Tessa was the first person Chris turned to for moral support or advice, as she always seemed to be able to put things into perspective. She was just mulling over in her head what she was going to say to that bunch of irritating morons tomorrow when the door to the wine bar opened and Tessa swung in.

Tessa was slightly shorter than Chris, with dark hair and a heart-shaped face. She looked around the room until she caught sight of Chris, and then, flashing a broad smile under her warm brown eyes, hurried up to her.

"Chrissie! Good to see you," she cried, taking her jacket off and hanging it on the back of a chair. "I was beginning to think you'd turned into a hermit! It feels like ages since we got together. What are you drinking? My shout."

Chris beamed at Tessa and stood up to greet her, hugging her tightly and planting a kiss on her cheek. "Pinot Grigio," she replied, "but let me get this round."

She started towards the bar but Tessa held up her hand to stop her.

"Sit down, sweetie. This calls for a bottle and I won't take no for an answer."

She grinned, and in a flash was up at the bar ordering. Chris watched her from her seat. Her easy grace as she chatted up the young, good-looking barman only served to make Chris more aware of her own awkwardness around men. Deep down she was a tiny bit envious of Tessa, who always had an endless stream of boyfriends, but she was so easy to talk to and genuinely seemed to care about her.

At university it had always been Tessa who had dragged her to parties and social gatherings. Her zest for fun seemed never ending and Chris had been caught up in her exuberance, although she was always the shy, quiet one at her side that no-one seemed to notice much. People appeared to like her, but felt more at ease with Tessa. Tessa never deserted her though and tried repeatedly to include Chris in every conversation, however short lived her success.

Chris was pulled out of her reminiscence by the sound of a bottle being plonked firmly on the table, and Tessa similarly plonking herself onto the seat opposite.

"OK, sweetie," she said, leaning towards her, "what's up? I can always tell when you're worried about something. You could never fool me."

Chris looked into her kind brown eyes and immediately felt more relaxed.

"My boss gave me my first solo assignment today and, although I know I can do it, I'm as nervous as hell. What if I mess up? What if I let him down and he decides that I'm a complete idiot? Half of me is excited at finally having the chance to do something real instead of just shadowing him, but the other half of me is in complete panic mode!"

She said the whole of that statement without pausing for breath and Tessa laughed at her.

"That's rubbish," she exclaimed. "You'll be absolutely fine. You were always far more studious than me and passed all your exams with flying colours. If I can manage to do a good job you certainly can. You just need to keep calm and do what you were trained to do." She poured out two glasses of wine and pushed the fresh glass towards Chris. "Get that down you and tell me exactly what part of the assignment worries you the most. You never know, I might be able to help."

Chris picked up her glass and, after downing almost half of it, relaxed into her chair and smiled apologetically at Tessa.

"Sorry about that," she said, raising her eyebrows. "It's that bloody art department. I ask them to do a simple job; one that they should be able to do with their eyes shut, and they give me grief! It happens every time I have to go in there. I don't know why I let them get to me. They're like sharks smelling blood when I enter the room. So they've done some bloody art degree. Doesn't make them gods."

Tessa laughed again.

"You need to be firmer, sweetie. You're good at what you do and they need to learn some respect." She refilled Chris's glass, which had almost been drained. "That boss of yours must think you're ready for the responsibility or he wouldn't trust you with such an important task. You really need to believe in yourself more."

"Easier said than done," Chris sighed.

Tessa burst into more laughter and, eyeing the near-empty bottle of wine on the table, remarked: "Time for some Chapman therapy I think. It's still early and my flat mates are having a 'drinks and nibbles' party this evening. I sort of said I'd be there, but their idea of party guests can sometimes be a bore; they're so intellectual. At least they like to think they are! You'll be doing me a huge favour by coming with me and giving me someone normal to talk to. We can sneak into my room with some nibbles and a couple of glasses of wine and dish the dirt. It'll be fun. What do you say?"

She was already putting her coat on and tugging at Chris's arm. Tessa was difficult to say no to when she was determined.

Chris thought about the empty flat she could go back to. Another night spent on her own watching rubbish TV with a ready-meal was really no competition for a lively evening with her best friend.

"OK," she replied "but I really can't stay too long. If I'm late tomorrow Feldman will definitely regret his decision and may even decide to fire me!"

She noted the look of triumph on Tessa's face, put her coat on and allowed herself be hustled towards the door.

It was then that she first noticed him.

He was on his own, leaning against the bar and staring at the door. It must have been raining outside because his thick dark hair was wet and there were droplets of water on his leather jacket. He abruptly turned back to the bar and picked up his drink. He was tall and of average build, smartly dressed, not bad looking really, Chris thought. But at that moment she heard Tessa calling impatiently to her, so she turned away and walked out into the street.

She thought no more about him.

Outside it was indeed raining, so they decided to take a taxi. It did not take them long to get to the flat in Pimlico as rush hour had long since subsided. Tessa opened the door with her key and ushered Chris in.

"I'm in your debt for this," she whispered. "Welcome to academia!"

Back at the wine bar the young man finished his drink and returned his gaze towards the door, where he saw a familiar face framed in the doorway. Tim Meyers smiled in acknowledgement and walked over to join him.

CHAPTER 5

The next morning Chris awoke to the sound of her alarm clock, followed shortly by the telephone ringing. Today was so important to her that to be on the safe side she had asked Tessa to call her, knowing that her friend was an habitual early riser.

She had always found this an annoying trait at university when they shared digs, but now she thanked heaven for it. Stumbling across the room and into the hallway, rubbing the sleep from her eyes, she grabbed the phone.

"Hello," she answered sleepily.

"Hello, sleepyhead," said a far too bubbly voice at the other end. "Time to get up and take on the world. Can't stop, got a train to catch and I haven't had breakfast yet, but phone me later and let me know how you got on. I've every faith in you, sweetie. Bye."

Chris grunted an incoherent reply and put the phone down.

"Coffee," she muttered, shuffling towards the kitchen, squinting and running her hand through her tousled hair, "and lots of it!"

The Victoria Line was as delightful as ever, but when she stepped out of Green Park station the sun was shining quite brightly and it looked as if at least the weather was going to be on her side today. She breezed through the doors of the office building and shot her customary smile at Tim. His eyes automatically went to the clock.

"Looks like you win today, Miss Newman," he grinned at her. "Mr Feldman's not in yet."

Chris flashed him a tolerant grin and walked straight to the lifts. How was that boy so cheerful in the mornings, she wondered, as the doors opened?

She swept past the marketing team, ignoring the surprised looks. Once in her office, she settled herself down and began analysing the list of companies her boss had given her. She started to make a plan of attack for each one.

As she had never done cold calling before this was going to need a bit of thought and preparation. She had read the background notes on each company yesterday, but needed to refresh her memory. As she glanced through them again and began rehearsing her opening gambit, Simon Feldman walked past her door, asking his secretary for some coffee before going into his office. He hung up his coat and picked up the post on his desk, which his secretary had opened and sorted for him.

Chris sighed. He was always so formal with her. Perhaps if she could show him that she was able to handle the job as well as he did, he would feel more relaxed around her. She got up and followed him in.

"Good morning," she said cheerily. He looked up at her and,

glancing at the clock on his wall, raised an eyebrow.

"I'm impressed, Miss Newman," he declared. "Looks like Big Ben is out of a job today." He started to read one of his letters.

"I briefed the art department yesterday and they're working on the updated presentation," she continued, unperturbed by his sarcasm. "I'll check on them shortly, but first I'll start contacting the names on my list. By this afternoon I should hopefully have some meetings lined up."

She paused for a reply. He continued reading the letter without looking up

"Fine, keep me informed," he casually responded.

Realising that she was going to get no further conversation from him, Chris acknowledged his request and turned to go back to her desk, muttering under her breath as she went: "You're welcome!"

She began the morning by telephoning the contacts on her list. The first two she called were too busy to talk, but their secretaries took her name and number and said they would pass them on to their respective bosses. Chris knew that they probably would not bother following up on a sales call, so made a note to call them back tomorrow.

The third target seemed more interested, but said he was going to be in Scotland for a few days on business. If she called next week he would be glad to set up a meeting.

She was feeling a bit dejected as she picked up the receiver to call the last name on her list. It was a company specialising in textiles, based in Sittingbourne. The phone rang at the other end and was answered by a female voice.

"Good morning, Taylor-Wood. How can I help you?"

Chris took a deep breath.

"Yes, good morning," she began. "Could I speak to Colin Matthews please? I believe he's the person in charge of your marketing department."

The woman on the other end of the phone paused briefly before answering.

"Yes, that's right," she replied. "One moment please and I'll check if he's in. May I ask who's calling?" Chris told her and waited patiently. "I'll just put you through now," she eventually heard the woman say. There was another brief pause before she heard a man's voice answer.

"Hello, Colin Matthews speaking," he said in a relaxed, welcoming tone. "How can I help you?"

Sounds friendly enough, Chris thought as she cleared her throat.

"Hello Mr Matthews, my name is Christina Newman from Feldman & Son," she began, trying to sound equally as friendly. "I'm not sure if you've heard of us, but we are an experienced, family-run marketing company that specialises in helping companies to reach potential new buyers for their products, particularly overseas.

"I know that your company has made quite a name for itself in the UK recently, and is now one of the country's leading manufacturers of quality silk scarves and ties. However, it seems that you haven't yet ventured abroad. I wondered if you could spare me some time to discuss the possibilities of extending your success to other countries. We have an established network of marketing outlets worldwide and I feel that, with our vast experience, we could be of help to you in getting your products to a wider audience."

She closed her eyes briefly and took a gulp of fresh air, hoping that she had not sounded too pushy or stuffy, or indeed come across as rambling. The reply surprised her.

"Actually," he replied. "I would be very interested in hearing why you think your company would be useful to us. Unfortunately, I'm tied up today and tomorrow, but I could see you on Monday morning at, shall we say, eleven. I need to leave the office by noon, but I'm sure that will leave you plenty of time to state your case."

Chris sighed in relief.

"Thank you, Mr Matthews. I'm sure I can convince you that our services would be very beneficial to you. I'll see you at eleven on Monday. Have a good weekend and thank you for your time," she said, before replacing the receiver and leaning back in her chair. "Wow," she thought. "My first solo appointment."

Glowing with excitement, she got up and knocked on Simon's door. He was on the phone but he beckoned her in.

"Thank you, Mr Hurst. I'll see you then," he was saying, as she crossed to his desk. He put the phone down and turned to her expectantly.

"I didn't have much luck with the first two names on my list," she informed him, "and the third one wants me to call him next week. However, I've managed to get an appointment on Monday morning to see Colin Matthews at Taylor-Wood in Sittingbourne."

Her voice rose slightly in pitch as she delivered the news of her single success, unable to contain her feeling of satisfaction.

"I wondered if you had any particular advice about how I should handle the meeting, seeing as it's my first solo one on behalf of the company."

Simon smiled. It amused him to see how enthusiastic she was. He remembered his own first attempts at getting new business. His awkwardness with people had been a bit of a handicap, but he had become used to it now. It was easier when he did not have to have daily contact with them.

"Well done," he congratulated her. "That's the first hurdle over, the next part might not be quite so easy though."

He noticed the worried look that crossed Chris's face and beckoned her to sit down.

"The trick is not to make them feel you are lecturing or pressurising them," he reassured her. "They are busy people and you need to be confident but respectful, after all they are experts in their field too. Make sure you read all there is to know about the company you are visiting before you go there, so that you can make your prospective client feel that you really do have their interests at heart. Be pleasant but not sycophantic. Above all, be concise – don't waffle. They'll be looking at their watches otherwise."

He raised an eyebrow and waited for her reaction.

"I'm sure I can manage that," she replied, smiling at him. "I've already read the file on them from the research department, but I'll look them up on the Internet as well, just to be on the safe side. Did you have any luck with your list?"

He looked down at the notes on his desk.

"As a matter of fact," he replied "I managed to go one better than you and have got two appointments planned. Mine are both for tomorrow. Did you get the presentation sorted? I'll need a copy for first thing in the morning"

Chris shuddered silently. In her eagerness to make a start on her calls, she had forgotten that, as there had been nothing in her emails when she got in, she still needed to visit the art department to chase it up.

"They promised me that they would email a proof to us this morning. It hadn't arrived when I last checked, so I'll go and see how they're doing now."

She smiled, hoping that he had not detected her oversight, and quickly left his office. Making her way reluctantly down the corridor, she braced herself in preparation to do battle.

Brad was not at his desk when she entered the room, but the other two were. They looked up when they heard her come in.

"Where's Brad?" she asked, looking at Sue.

"He's making himself a coffee," came the reply, just as Brad came through the door behind Chris. She turned at the sound of his footsteps.

"Ah, Miss Newman," he exclaimed, over-stressing her name and holding her gaze in an attempt to make her blush. He crossed to his desk and carefully put his coffee down. "Your presentation, I presume!"

Chris ignored his provocative tone and drew herself up to her full height.

"You said it would be ready for us to check by this morning," she said looking him squarely in the eyes. "Mr Feldman and I both have appointments over the next few days, so we will definitely be needing the final copy."

Brad looked at her and smiled, seeing through her display of feigned authority.

"Luckily for you we are all geniuses in this department and have produced an excellent presentation," he retorted. He waited for a response to his remark, but Chris decided not to rise to the bait.

"No need to applaud," he continued sarcastically. "We're used to being taken for granted here. I've just emailed a copy to both you and Feldman."

"Thank you," Chris replied. "I'm sure it will be exactly to the standard we expect of you. I'll let you know when it's been approved so that you can burn the CDs and finalise the hard copies."

She then turned on her heels and breezed out of the room. This time she did hear Sue's faint giggle.

It was nearly time for lunch, so she decided to go out and grab her usual take-away sandwich and eat it at her desk while she checked the presentation. After opening her emails to make sure she had received the file from Brad, she knocked on Simon's door, to ask if he wanted anything to eat. Discovering that he was having lunch with a client, she returned to her office, put on her coat and grabbed her bag. She made her way down in the lift and left the building. As she passed Tim, he looked up, smiled and watched her go out. Then he picked up the phone.

"She's just leaving the office," he said, and replaced the receiver.

* * * * * *

Chris made her way down the street to one of the local sandwich bars. The sun was quite warm now and she wished she had left her coat in the office. A queue had built up, but the waiting time gave her a chance to think about which sandwich she wanted today.

When she finally got to the front, the man behind the counter smiled at her. She had found this particular sandwich bar on her first day at the company, admiring the range of fillings and bread that it offered. As she now came here most days, he recognised her immediately.

"What can I get for you today?" he beamed.

"I'll have a tuna mayo sandwich on granary and a cappuccino, please," she replied, smiling back at him.

He made her sandwich up and got her a cappuccino. Thanking him and paying, she turned to leave and promptly collided with someone behind her depositing most of her coffee onto the floor.

"Oh," she cried, "I'm so sorry."

Looking at the stranger's face, she found herself staring into a pair of deep blue eyes. The handsome man looking down at her seemed vaguely familiar, although she could not think why. She only knew that she seemed to have spilt some of the coffee on his jacket and felt embarrassed.

"No, my fault entirely," he replied. "Please let me get you another one."

Chris protested immediately.

"Oh no, I couldn't let you do that. I wasn't looking where I was going. It's fine, really."

The man shook his head and insisted.

"I won't take no for an answer," he declared, and turning to the sandwich man, who had started to mop up the coffee on the floor, ordered another cappuccino and one for himself.

Chris rummaged around in her mind to remember where she had seen the man before, but the recollection evaded her. He handed her the coffee and they walked outside together.

"My name is Mark, by the way. Mark Dempster." He held out his hand, then, realising that Chris had both hands occupied by her coffee and the sandwich, he smiled. "Sorry, I'm being extremely clumsy today. I'm not usually like this, I promise."

Chris smiled back awkwardly. He was gazing straight into her eyes and she found that she had lost the use of speech. Why did this always happen when she got anywhere near a good-looking guy? No wonder she was still unattached. She really had to get a grip of herself.

"I think you'll find that I'm the clumsy one," she said, "but thank you for this." She held up the coffee, trying to look relaxed and casual. "I'm Chris. Chris Newman."

She put the sandwich into her coat pocket and held out her hand to him. He shook it and held on to it, without breaking eye contact. Chris began to feel a little uneasy and, as if sensing it, he let go of her hand.

"I'm afraid I have to dash off," he said. "I need to be somewhere, but it was a pleasure 'bumping into you', Chris."

Remembering that she needed to check over the presentation and that her lunch hour was slipping away, Chris hurried back to the office.

Mark stopped around the corner and watched her walk in the opposite direction. He smiled smugly to himself, then turned and walked away.

CHAPTER 6

The afternoon passed quickly.

Chris checked the presentation, made sure that Simon had received his copy by email and then spent some time looking up Taylor-Wood on the Internet. They had an impressive site and she made some notes to check against those she already had on file. They appeared to be an ideal candidate for the Italian market, as their silk products were at the high-end of the fashion scale. She decided to do some research into the best way of promoting the company in Italy and which specific areas to target.

Her Italian was pretty much non-existent, so she decided to ask her boss for some help, given his Italian connections. He was not going to be around much tomorrow, so she knocked on his open door to see if she could pick his brains before he went home. He was signing letters that his secretary had typed up for him.

"Come in," he said, gesturing towards the chair in front of his desk. "How's it going? I've looked at the presentation. They've done quite a good job on it, far better than their last effort. I couldn't find any mistakes so you can tell them to get on with the hard copies and CDs. You've obviously made an impression on them."

He smiled at her. She was not sure if he was making fun of her or not, but decided to take it as a compliment.

"I don't think that's the case," she replied modestly, sitting down. "It was probably more that they knew you wanted a copy that made the difference.

"I've just been checking out Taylor-Wood's profile on their website and it seems to me that Italy would be a good market for them, to start with anyway. Their products would sell really well there. I know that it's your area of expertise, so I wondered if there was anything I should be aware of before I start recommending that route to the client? Also my Italian is pretty non-existent."

Simon put down his pen and leaned back in his chair.

"We have an office in Rome, so I would speak to them first," he suggested. "They have dealings with all the main advertising outlets and importing companies and are involved with all the major trade fairs, so they'll be able to give you all the help you need. Talk to Antonio Mancini, he runs the office. He's a nice guy and he speaks perfect English. His number is in the contacts file on the intranet and also on our website."

He waited for Chris to finish making notes.

"By the way," he continued, "I won't be in at all tomorrow. My first appointment is in north London but the second is in Guildford, so I've decided to stay with my parents for the weekend, in Esher. I'll go straight there after the meeting."

Chris wished him luck and a good weekend and then went back to her office to ring Antonio. She knew it might be a little premature, not having even clinched the deal, but she wanted to at least be able to sound confident of her facts. She picked up the receiver before realising that they were an hour ahead in Rome, so, as it was already nearly five o'clock UK-time, there would probably be no one there.

"A job for tomorrow," she thought, and put the receiver down again.

* * * * * * *

When Chris got back to her flat that evening the light on the answer phone in the hallway was flashing.

It was her mother. She rolled her eyes and sat down on the chair by the side of the phone.

"Hello, dear, it's your mother," the voice said. "Your father and I thought we had better let you know that we're still alive as we haven't heard from you recently. If you still have the use of your arms please call us back…soon!"

The message ended and Chris sighed. Her parents meant well but since her younger brother, Adam, had gone to university they had found the house in Oxford a bit empty. Now that they only had each other for company, her mother in particular had become far too interested in her life, deciding that it was unnatural for a girl of Chris's age not to be dating anyone.

"I'm not taking on the full force of my mother without something to eat," she thought and went into the kitchen. The freezer offered the usual bland selection of frozen dinners, but she took out a lasagne and popped it into the microwave just the same.

She changed into her jeans and a T-shirt, then, after pouring herself a glass of wine, grabbed the now heated meal, took it into the lounge and settled down to eat straight from the carton.

Wonderful – another evening on her own! Perhaps her mother was right, maybe she was odd. Her friends never seemed to have any difficulty in getting dates, although some of their choices were admittedly dubious. She switched on the TV and flicked through the channels. The usual cavalcade of rubbish greeted her.

Finishing the lasagne, she returned to the kitchen, put the empty carton in the rubbish bin and washed up her fork. Clutching her glass for moral support, she picked up the phone and dialled her parents' number. "Might as well get it over with," she told herself.

The ringing tone at the other end was interrupted by her father's voice.

"Hello," he said, then on hearing that it was Chris immediately replied, "I'll get your mother, dear."

He was a man of few words and had always found communication with his daughter difficult. Years of being dominated by his overbearing wife had made him wary of any kind of discourse with a female. Chris wondered if she got her awkwardness from him. She tried to engage him in conversation but he had gone before she could get the words out. Soon her mother was taking charge of the phone.

"There you are at last," she said pointedly. "We were beginning to think that you'd developed amnesia and forgotten you have parents. Is it too much to ask for a phone call, even just once a week, to let us know you're OK? I so miss the little chats we used to have before you moved to London, and your father is no company at all. Always in that damn shop of his, or with his head in a book."

She paused for dramatic effect. Chris rolled her eyes again. Her mother was such a drama queen.

"I'm fine, mother," she replied, trying not to convey her annoyance. "I've been really busy at work. I've finally been given my own assignment and I don't want to mess it up. It's my chance to show my worth. It's a brilliant opportunity. You should be pleased. You're always telling me that I should assert myself more."

"I meant in the boyfriend department, dear," her mother huffed. "Susan Harris was only asking me this morning in the staff room if you were seeing anyone yet. Her daughter Megan has just announced her engagement to an absolutely charming man. Apparently they were childhood sweethearts and he's now making quite a name for himself in the City."

Chris groaned. Her mother was a teacher and constantly made Chris feel as if she was one of her pupils, being forced to make excuses for her behaviour. Why did the conversation always have to end up about boys anyway?

"I'm perfectly happy as I am, mother," she snapped. "I'm only 25. I need to enjoy my life before I settle down. There's so much I want to do first."

Her mother sniffed.

"You'll be left on the shelf if you leave it too long, my girl. You don't even seem to want to date anyone. That would be a start. I worry about you, Christina, I really do. So does your father."

Chris doubted that. Her poor father probably had not even been allowed to venture an opinion.

"When are we going to see you, dear?" her mother continued, not waiting for her daughter to comment.

"Soon, I hope mother," Chris replied. "It will depend on how my appointment goes on Monday. If the client wants to engage our services then I will probably be tied up for a while, but I promise I'll come up to Oxford as soon as I can."

She hoped her mother would not pursue the matter, as she was rapidly tiring of this particular line of interrogation.

"I wish your father hadn't insisted on getting that flat for you," her mother moaned. "You're becoming far too self-contained. I feel you don't need us anymore."

Chris could visualise her pouting on the other end of the line.

"Don't do that, mother," she sighed. "Self pity really doesn't suit you. I'll call again soon. Love to daddy."

Her mother sniffed in indignation.

"You're becoming quite hard Christina. It doesn't suit you either. Bye."

The phone clicked as her mother hung up. She could be so infuriating, even from a distance.

Chris went back to the sofa and tried to concentrate on the television, which was still playing away to itself. It was one of those dreadful quiz shows. What did people see in them, she thought?

After flicking between the channels and finding nothing better to watch, she got up and retrieved her laptop. Accessing Facebook, she trawled through her home page to see what had been happening in her absence and then entered Tessa's profile. Noting that all of her recent entries had been posted during the afternoon, she raised her eyebrows and wondered exactly what Tessa did all day that allowed her to find the time for gossiping.

Chuckling, she then decided that it would be nice to arrange another night out with her. It was Friday tomorrow so she would not have to worry about work the next day.

The thought pleased her and, typing a comment to that effect on Tessa's wall, she settled down to let the rest of the evening wash over her.

CHAPTER 7

Chris began the next day by phoning the first two contacts she had tried the day before but still could not get to talk to them. Their secretaries were like Rottweilers.

Then she called Antonio in Rome and had a long conversation with him. Simon was right, his English was excellent and he turned out to be extremely helpful. She made lots of notes and added them to her Taylor-Wood file.

Finally, she called Tessa and made arrangements to meet her in Toppers after work. They could decide then what to do for the rest of the evening.

Simon called after his first appointment, to see if there was anything that needed his attention before he went to his second meeting. The north London contact had been interested but not yet ready to commit to overseas investment. He was hoping that his next meeting would be more fruitful. Chris wished him luck again and returned to her own thoughts of success for the rest of the day.

She left the office, saying goodnight to Tim on the way out, and walked over to the wine bar. She did not notice Tim accompanying her departure with his, by now, customary phone call.

Toppers was beginning to fill up as people began to celebrate the start of the weekend, so Chris had to wait to be served at the bar. She finally managed to order a bottle of wine and found a table. Tessa had warned that she might be a bit late getting there, so she poured herself a glass and started reading a book that she had brought with her. She became so engrossed that she did not see Mark approaching her.

"Hello, again," he said, making her jump. "I'm sorry, I seem to be making a habit out of startling you. I saw you sitting here on your own and thought I'd take the chance to apologise properly for yesterday. The coffee incident?" He smiled at her and once again she found herself captivated by his blue eyes.

"Oh yes, it's Mark isn't it," she replied. "There's really no need, it's me who should be offering to pay for your dry cleaning bill. I'm actually waiting for someone but she said she's going to be a bit late." She glanced towards the door, but there was still no sign of Tessa. "Would you like a glass of wine? I can at least offer you that."

Mark accepted her invitation and sat down opposite her, picking up the glass she had poured for him. As he took a sip, Chris suddenly realised where she had seen him before. He was the man she had noticed at the bar the other evening as she was leaving.

"Now that I come to think of it," she remarked, already feeling surprisingly relaxed in his company, "I'm sure I saw you here, at the bar, on Wednesday evening. Is this your local?"

"Not really," he replied, smiling. "I haven't been in the area long, I move around a lot, but it seems quite a nice place. How about you? I'm guessing you work locally, judging by your visit to the sandwich bar. Which company do you work for?"

He leaned back in his chair. There was a sudden burst of laughter from a group of men by the bar, which momentarily distracted Chris.

"I'm sorry," he continued, "I'm not normally this pushy, it's just that I don't know many people and you're easy to talk to. I hope you don't mind my questions."

Chris could not quite believe that someone was actually taking an interest in her, and suddenly she felt self-conscious. It was usually Tessa who drew people towards her. She was used to being the shy, boring friend. This was a new experience.

"Of course not," she said quickly, not wanting to frighten him off. "I work just around the corner, for Feldman & Son. I'm Mr Feldman's assistant. We're a marketing company. I don't suppose you've heard of us?"

He raised an eyebrow.

"Actually, I have. I've had dealings with them in the past." His expression momentarily darkened, but he checked himself and smiled. "Which Mr Feldman do you work with? Senior or junior?"

Chris did not notice the change.

"Junior," she replied. "Simon Feldman. His father had to retire because of ill health, I believe. It was before I joined so I never knew him. Why do you ask? Did you deal with them both?"

Mark was quiet for a moment.

"I was only associated with the company through a third party," he finally said, "but it was Feldman senior who was involved in the deal. I don't really know much about either of them."

His gaze drifted reflectively past her into space, as if he was lost in his own thoughts. Once again he pulled himself together.

"I know this may seem a bit of a thin chat up line," he said suddenly, smiling at her, "but I don't suppose you'd have dinner with me tomorrow night – if you haven't anything else planned for the weekend that is? I'll understand if you'd rather not, but it would be nice to get to know you, now that we've formally introduced ourselves, so to speak."

Chris was taken aback. It had been quite a while since she had been on a date with a guy. That was at university, and it had not gone well. Both of them had quickly discovered they had nothing in common and spent the evening desperately trying to think of excuses to leave. She was not in a particular hurry to repeat the experience, but something about Mark intrigued her.

"I'd love to," she replied, giving him her best smile but trying not to appear too eager.

Just then Tessa breezed into the bar and, after looking around the room, saw Chris and waved.

"My friend is here now," Chris exclaimed, seeing her and waving back, "but you can join us if you like."

Mark looked over his shoulder and, seeing Tessa descending upon them, stood up.

"I'm afraid I can't stay," he said, turning back to Chris, "but can I have your address and I'll pick you up tomorrow evening at about seven-thirty. You'd better let me have your phone number too."

Chris rummaged in her bag and pulled out a scrap of paper. She hastily wrote down both her mobile and landline numbers, and handed them to Mark.

"Thanks," he said, putting the paper in his pocket. "I'll see you tomorrow. Have a good evening." With that he turned and walked away, passing and ignoring Tessa. As he reached the door and disappeared outside, Chris realised she had not asked for his number. "Damn," she exclaimed under her breath.

"Who was that?" Tessa asked as she reached Chris, following Mark with her eyes. "He's pretty hot!"

Chris rolled her eyes.

"You needn't sound so surprised," she remarked, feigning a hurt expression. "You make it sound as if I'm totally incapable of attracting a man."

Tessa laughed, raised her eyebrows, then took off her coat and sat down.

"I didn't mean it like that, sweetie," she cooed. "It's just that I've never seen you show any serious interest in a guy before, especially the guys I've tried to introduce you to. The minute I turn my back there you are not only engaging a hot one in conversation, but presumably giving him your number!"

Chris smiled at her, caught the eye of a passing waiter and asked him for another glass.

"That's because you always want to pair me up with really nerdy guys or lads who need mothering," she replied, "neither of whom I have the slightest interest in. Besides, Mark is just being kind. I literally bumped into him yesterday. I spilt coffee over his jacket and now *he* wants to take *me* to dinner to say sorry. It should really be me taking him!"

The waiter arrived with the fresh glass, and while Chris poured, Tessa proceeded to recount her day. Chris listened attentively but could not help letting her mind wander back to Mark. She still found it hard to understand why a complete stranger would be so keen to buy her dinner, and what the hell was she going to talk to him about? All they seemed to have in common so far was coffee! Tessa's voice filtered back into her mind and she promptly dismissed Mark from it until tomorrow night.

Outside, Mark took the piece of paper out of his pocket and studied the address – Ebury Street, Victoria. He was relieved it was in town and easy to get to. He had been an idiot not to ask her where she lived before committing himself. He could have ended up travelling miles just to get the information he wanted.

Still, no harm done. Fortunately, she had turned out to be pretty good-looking and reasonably intelligent, so at the very least it looked as if he would enjoy himself. He smiled at the thought and put the paper back in his pocket. This was possibly going to be easier than he had imagined.

He strolled down the road, whistling contentedly to himself.

CHAPTER 8

Simon Feldman's afternoon in Guildford had gone well. The meeting with his second potential client had shown all the signs of a lucrative deal and by the time Simon had gone through the presentation, explained all the possible areas in which his company could be of help, met with the people who would be involved on the marketing side and agreed another meeting to discuss specifics, it was six o'clock.

He had phoned his mother that morning to let her know that he would be staying for the weekend and she had received the news with obvious delight.

"That's wonderful, darling," she exclaimed. "Your father and I see so little of you these days. It'll be so nice to spend some time catching up. I'll get Anna to cook something special tonight as a treat. What time do you think you can get here?" Simon told her that he hoped to be with them by about seven o'clock, but that he would phone when he was on his way.

At just after seven, he drove his silver-grey Porsche up the wide driveway to his parents' home, a large six-bedroom house with extensive grounds. As he approached it, he wondered why they still felt the need for such a huge house, even with a gardener and housekeeper to maintain it. After all, it was not as if they entertained much these days and he was certainly not planning on getting married or presenting them with any grandchildren in the near future.

Parking in front of the garage, he got out, took his case and laptop bag out of the boot and walked towards the house. His mother, Caroline, was waiting for him at the large front door, surrounded by a profusion of hanging baskets and planters. She hugged him warmly and ushered him in.

"Your father's in his study as usual," she said, sighing. "He's supposed to be resting but he says he gets bored doing nothing. Perhaps now that you're here he'll relax a bit."

Simon kissed her on the cheek, put his bags down in the hallway, hung up his jacket and walked towards his father's study, gently tapping on the door.

"Come in," came the reply, upon which Simon opened the door and stepped inside. It was a large room, formerly a library, which his father had turned into an office several years ago so that he could work from home. The walls were still lined with bookshelves, which were well stocked with a variety of reference books, files and novels. Two large filing cabinets sat neatly in one of the corners, on top of which sat a pot plant. His father was sitting at a large mahogany desk by the French windows, reading some papers. He had a few books stacked up around him, one or two of which lay open. On seeing

Simon he smiled and started to get up.

Simon hurried over and put his hand on his father's shoulder, stopping him from rising.

"Don't get up dad, you need to conserve your energy," he said. "What are you doing in here anyway? You know the doctor said you should rest and not over exert yourself, and you know how much mother worries about you. Besides, I'm here now so you can relax and talk to me."

"The doctor and your mother fuss too much, Simon," harrumphed his father. "I simply get out of breath easily, that's all. I've got emphysema – I'm not a total invalid. I just have to be careful, and I am."

His wife appeared at the door to inform them both that dinner was ready. Simon went to help his father get up, but was waved away. Daniel rose, wheezing slightly, and led the way into the dining room.

After dinner, Caroline left the two men talking in the lounge while she went off to the kitchen to organise some coffee. Daniel proceeded to quiz his son on affairs at the office, and how business was going. He was very keen to know if any new business had been brought in, but also wanted to be sure that the regular clients were still happy.

Simon patiently answered every question. He was painfully aware that his father still remembered his reluctance to take over the business, even though Simon had agreed it was necessary, given the circumstances. He regretted that his then lack of enthusiasm meant that his father now felt the need to check up on him all the time. He felt a desperate desire to prove to his father that, not only did he care, but he was also in control.

"I have an excellent assistant now, dad," he said intently, "and between us we are knocking on doors. You know we discussed turning our attention to the UK market more, well it seems that there's definitely potential there. My assistant, Christina Newman, seems to have drummed up some interest from a company in Sittingbourne and I have a couple of irons in the fire. It's early days yet but it's quite an exciting prospect. We're a good team and I'm on top of things, so you really don't need to worry."

His father's face, on hearing him mention Chris's name, instantly changed to a look of concern.

"Simon," he exclaimed, "I hope you're maintaining a professional relationship with this girl, especially if, as I suspect, she's young and pretty. I know what an eye for the girls you have, and personally I think you've been wise to play the field before finding the right girl – even though your mother is desperate for you to settle down. However, it's never a good idea to get too intimate with your staff."

Simon was slightly taken aback at his father's unprovoked outburst.

"I'm always totally business-like with my staff, dad," he exclaimed, with a look of indignation. "I conduct myself as professionally as possible. Christina is good at her job and I treat her accordingly."

His father smiled indulgently at him. He was proud of his son and expected great things of him, just as his father had of him. Except that Thomas Feldman had been a much harder man to please than himself. He watched his son trying desperately to impress him and let his mind wander back to the days of his own youth, when he too had been young and full of ideas. However, Thomas had not been interested in seeking his advice, he had only required his unquestioning obedience. He remembered all the harsh words and pointless arguments between them and was determined that his relationship with Simon was not going to go down that route.

"I'm sure you have everything under control, Simon. I just get so bored here, not being caught up in the day-to-day whirl of things. I know I can't actively get involved anymore but I still like to feel part of it all. Being kept informed is the next best thing."

He smiled at Simon, who gave him a look of concern as he started to cough. Daniel held up his hand to reassure him.

"I'm fine," he huffed. "It just catches me occasionally. Your mother thinks we should spend some time at the vineyard in Tuscany so that I can 'breathe in some good air' as she puts it. I still have one or two cousins there who we keep in contact with. I must admit it would be nice to see the old place again. It's been years since I was last there." He seemed lost in his own thoughts for a while and then returned his gaze to Simon.

"I was always very happy there with your grandmother's parents," he continued, thoughtfully. "As a child they spoilt me rotten, which made a change from the way my father treated me. He never found it easy to show his feelings, especially with me. He was better with your aunt Sophia, but I suppose that's natural with a daughter. He didn't expect so much of her."

Simon's mother came back into the room with the coffee and the conversation turned away from nostalgia and business to lighter topics.

CHAPTER 9

The next morning Simon did not wake until nine o'clock, which was unusual for him as he was generally an early riser. He had obviously needed the sleep, but now that the sun streamed through the closed curtains he was wide awake.

He jumped out of bed, took a shower, dressed and, on coming down from his room, found his mother in the kitchen discussing lunch with Anna, her cook and housekeeper. She smiled at him and instructed Anna to get her son some breakfast.

"Good morning, darling," she said kissing his cheek. "Your father and I have already had our breakfast. He's in the conservatory reading the paper. When you've finished eating you can join him. I have some things to do this morning so he'll be glad of the company. Please try and persuade him to go to Italy, he might listen to you. Make him see that the company is not going to collapse just because he's out of the country for a week or so. You know how stubborn he can be. I'll see you both later this afternoon."

With that she swept out of the kitchen and shortly afterwards Simon heard the front door close.

He quickly ate the breakfast Anna had put in front of him, then poured a mug of coffee for himself and carried it into the conservatory, where his father was sitting with his legs propped up on a footstool and a newspaper spread on his lap. He was gazing out onto the garden, but on hearing Simon's footsteps on the marble tiled floor he turned and gave him a broad smile.

"Good morning, son," he said, folding the newspaper and putting it down on the floor. "Did you sleep well? It looks as if it's going to be just the two of us for most of the day. Your mother has got herself involved with the local WI. I think she's helping to organise a bring-and-buy sale for the local church. Still, at least it will stop her worrying about me for a while."

Simon sat down in a chair beside him. Daniel wheezed a little, picked up an inhaler and breathed it in.

"What about you?" he continued. "Have you any plans for today?"

Simon finished his coffee and put the mug on the coffee table in front of him.

"I thought perhaps you and I could have lunch together," he suggested. "I know a nice pub by the river at Thames Ditton. It's not far away and it looks as if it's going to be a fine day. It will do you good to get some air and we really should make the most of the summer while it's here. My treat. What do you say?"

Daniel readily agreed. Since his illness he had been advised not to drive, so he rarely went out unless his wife drove and these days her time seemed to have been monopolised by the WI and various other local activities. He was glad in a way because she did have a tendency to exaggerate his incapacity, so the prospect of getting out of the house without the customary fuss was quite appealing. Besides, it would be a good opportunity to talk to his son, just the two of them. He had always been too busy with the company and his own distractions when Simon was growing up, and because of that his wife had always been the favoured parent. This had resulted in them becoming somewhat distant and awkward with each other. Recently he had had time to regret that, and now he felt he had a chance to do something about it.

Just after midday, Simon helped his father into his car and they drove out towards Thames Ditton. The sun was quite hot, so Simon wound the windows down to let some fresh air into the car. Daniel did not say very much during the journey. After commenting grumpily on the impracticality of his son's car for passengers, which brought a smile to Simon's face, he turned his attention to enjoying the ride and the countryside.

When they arrived at the pub it was already getting busy, but they managed to find a table on the terrace, by the river. The picturesque riverside pub was a popular place for families at the weekend and today was no exception.

After settling his father into a chair, Simon went into the bar and eventually brought out two pints of bitter. He found Daniel gazing dreamily at the boats slowly drifting along.

"I always fancied having a boat," he said, as Simon placed the drinks on the table and sat down. "But your grandfather thought that it was an extravagance and a possible distraction. He had very definite ideas about my future and how I should live my life. I thought the world of him but he wasn't always a kind man."

Simon looked at his father and saw sadness in his eyes. Now that he came to think of it, he had never heard his father talk about his past before, nor about anything outside of the company. Although he knew that his father loved him, there had always seemed to be an imaginary door between them, one that Daniel wanted to keep closed.

"You've never really talked to me much about grandfather," Simon ventured. "I can only remember him as an old man who gave me sweets, told me stories about Italy and gave me a rollicking if I was too noisy. What was he really like?"

Daniel gave a sudden wheeze and Simon instinctively reached out to help him but his father waved him off.

"I'm fine," he said reassuringly. "Just my lungs getting accustomed to the air." He took a sip of his beer and glanced back at the boats before continuing. "He fought in Italy, during World War II. He was with the Eighth Army, supporting the American Fifth Army in its capture of Rome in June 1944. He fell in love with the country, particularly Tuscany. After the war he decided to spend some time there and eventually met and married your grandmother, Gabriella, my mother. She was very beautiful and I adored her. So did my father, in his own way."

Daniel's face clouded a little at the thought.

"He had come from quite a poor East End family," he went on, "and was determined to make a better life for himself. My mother's family owned a small vineyard just outside the town of Monteriggioni and, although not exactly rich, they were quite comfortably off compared to a lot of people still recovering from the effects of the War. Wine was seen as a source of calories back then, and therefore important to the Italian diet. They were lucky."

A light breeze swept a few strands of his greying hair into his eyes and he absent-mindedly brushed them back into place.

"After they were married my parents moved in with my grandparents. Dad worked at the vineyard for a while, but it wasn't really his thing. Didn't fit into his grand plans. He had a good head for business and the daily routine wasn't exciting enough for him. He wanted to make a name for himself and he felt that he would stand a better chance back here, in London. So in 1948 he upped sticks and brought my mother back to England."

He took another sip of his drink and Simon noted the frown etched across his face.

"Was Gran happy to come here?" asked Simon, sensing disapproval in his father's tone. Daniel gave him a wry smile.

"Your grandfather was never that interested in what other people thought," he sniffed disapprovingly, "only what he wanted. But, my mother loved him unconditionally and she would have done anything for him, so she left her family and everything she knew and found herself in a strange country, with no friends and very little English. Many people treated her coldly at first – after all, her country had been the enemy only a few years previously. Fortunately, her beauty and easy charm gradually won them over and her English quickly improved."

By now a cloud had started to obscure the sun and the air was chilly. Worried that it might affect his father's chest, Simon suggested that they went inside to eat. Some people were leaving, so they did not have to wait long for a table. After ordering their food Simon was keen to resume their conversation, now that he sensed the door beginning to open.

"I know he must have been successful," he said, "because of how well the company is doing now, but did Gran see much of her family after that? She must have missed them."

"Your grandfather was a determined man," replied Daniel, "so it wasn't long before he managed to establish the company. After that they went back once a year for holidays. My father had made quite a few friends there during his stay in Tuscany, and they proved to be very useful to him when setting up links with Italy. He got the most out of every last one of them – he was never one to let friendship get in the way of business."

He smiled to himself as the waiter arrived with their meal.

Simon realised delving into his family's past had given him quite an appetite.

"Did you and Aunt Sophia spend much time there?" asked Simon. "I only have vague recollections of meeting my Italian great grandparents. I can't even remember what they looked like, but I think I remember the vineyard and somewhere that looked like a castle."

His father smiled at Simon's sketchy recollections.

"That would be the city walls and turrets of Monteriggioni," he confirmed. "It's a medieval town close to the vineyard. I used to love climbing the walls when I was a boy. I felt like the king of the world up there and the view was stunning. Your mother and I used to take you there when you were very young."

"Why did you stop going?" questioned Simon further. "You mentioned that we still have family there – cousins you said. How about aunts and uncles?"

Daniel pushed his empty plate to one side and sighed.

"They say we're all products of our parents. In my case I was very much moulded by my father. As I grew up he started to become interested in my … advancement." He stressed the last word and gave another wry smile. "He gradually took me over until I almost became an extension of him. Ruthless in business and totally self absorbed."

He gazed deep into Simon's eyes and his voice became earnest.

"Simon," he barked. "I have done a lot of things in my life that I'm not proud of and lately I have had ample time to reflect on them. Going back to Monteriggioni would only stir up memories I would rather forget."

The waiter came to clear their plates and so Simon ordered coffee. He turned back to Daniel, who was now staring out of the window.

"What did you do that was so bad?" he asked tentatively. "As long as I can remember you've always been this hard working man who lived for the company and his family."

Inwardly Simon was thinking that it was the company that had taken the lion's share of his father's time and attentions. In all honesty, he could not remember spending that much time with his father when he was younger. Only after he had left university, and his presence was deemed necessary to carry on the business, did he become the focus of attention.

Daniel slowly turned around to look at Simon and then tapped the table with both hands.

"OK," he snapped. "Enough of this trip down memory lane! Let's change the subject now."

Simon did not argue. He was pleased just that the door between them had been pushed ajar, even though it now appeared to have been firmly slammed shut once more.

CHAPTER 10

Chris overslept again on Saturday morning, having drunk far more than intended the night before.

Tessa had spoken non-stop about the latest man on her hit list. A new guy had just joined her company who, according to her, was "fit". She had spent the last couple of days trying to get him to ask her out but he seemed not to have noticed her come-ons. She was now plotting to fine-tune her seduction techniques.

"You probably scared the life out of him," Chris had teased her. "You can be a force of nature when you're in full flow!"

They had then left Toppers in search of somewhere to eat, finally going back to Tessa's flat, where they talked until well after midnight about men and their shortcomings. Lying in bed now, Chris felt as if she had died and nobody had thought to tell her.

Getting up slowly and carefully, she made her way to the bathroom and stared at herself in the mirror, groaning. Whoever was staring back at her looked just as bad as she felt, maybe even worse! Why did she always consume so much alcohol when she was with Tessa? She really must give up drinking for a while. Then she remembered agreeing to go to dinner with Mark and a wave of panic ran through her. She had until seven-thirty to turn into something human – a bit of a tall order, she thought.

After cleaning her teeth and showering she went back to her bedroom and threw on some casual clothes. She didn't really feel like eating any breakfast but knew that it would probably be wise to put something in her stomach, so she made herself some toast and coffee.

By now the sun was streaming in through the kitchen window. Shielding her eyes, she groaned again and pulled down the blind. As nice as it was to see the sunshine, her eyes were definitely not ready to meet it yet. She ate her toast in the kitchen, propping herself up against the sink unit, before taking her coffee into the living room, where she curled up on the sofa, moaning quietly to herself.

Last night Tessa had interrogated her about Mark and Chris realised she knew absolutely nothing about him. She did not even know where he lived. Now, in the cold light of day, she wondered if it had been wise to accept his invitation. Still, it was too late now and she could not even contact him to offer an excuse for baling out. She would just have to go through with it.

The rest of the day was spent getting her head in the right place, aided by copious amounts of coffee. When she felt able to face the outside world, she went food shopping, to stock up her freezer with more ready-meals, as well as a few basics.

"I really should have paid more attention in cookery class," she sighed as, back at the flat, she viewed her sorry frozen purchases and stashed them in the freezer.

Half way through putting the rest of the shopping away, the phone rang. Before she had time to talk, Tessa's excited voice chimed in.

"Sweetie," she exclaimed excitedly. "You'll never guess who just called me."

Chris waited a while, as if trying to think.

"Err… I've no idea Tess. Who was it?" she eventually replied.

"Peter from the office!" Tessa squealed. "How cool is that? Apparently, he got my number from Jill in accounts. He asked me if I'd like to see a film with him tonight and then go for a meal. It seems he likes me after all! I've no idea what I'm going to wear. I may have to hit the shops. Better go now, speak to you later, sweetie."

She squealed again.

Chris smiled to herself. Tessa was always so full-on about everything. She could not help thinking how different their reactions were to their impending dates. Once more she found herself wishing she could be more like Tessa.

By late afternoon Chris began to feel like her old self, and by the time she started to get ready for her date she was actually hungry.

Consulting her wardrobe and finding nothing that really inspired her, she settled on a plain black, slim-fitting dress with red piping. She put her hair up and did her make-up. She was going to feel decidedly overdressed if they ended up at McDonald's. She finished off the outfit with black high heels and went into the lounge, where she sat on the sofa to await her fate.

"You'll be fine, Christina," she told herself. "He's only a guy you happened to spill coffee on. Think of it as a business meeting. It'll be good practice."

At exactly seven-thirty the doorbell rang. Chris took a deep breath and when she opened it, Mark was standing there, dressed in dark grey trousers and a smart navy blazer. His white shirt was open at the neck. Chris smiled nervously. He returned the smile and produced a bunch of flowers from behind his back. He stepped into the hallway and closed the door behind him.

While she was in the kitchen, arranging the flowers in a glass vase, which she had finally managed to find in one of the cupboards, Mark went into the lounge and nosed around, taking in every detail from the pine floorboards to the abstract pictures on the pale walls. He noted that they complimented the smart modern furniture. "Nice," he thought to himself, turning his attention to the coffee table and picking up a book that was lying there. He read the cover and, noting that it was a romantic novel, smiled inwardly and placed it back on the table, just as Chris came into the room.

"Would you like a drink before we go," she asked him, hoping he would not want anything too specific as she only had a bottle of white wine in the fridge.

Luckily, he politely declined and suggested that they should go, as he had booked the restaurant for eight o'clock. Relieved, Chris picked up her jacket, which she had laid on the armchair ready, and he was by her side in a flash to help her put it on. A bit taken aback, she nevertheless allowed him to hold the jacket while she slipped her arms into it.

"Wow," she thought. "Such a gentleman. This guy has got to be too good to be true."

Mark had parked his car right outside the flat, despite the double yellow lines. "Well at least he's not a stickler for rules," she thought. He walked ahead of her, opened the door of the blue Mercedes Cabriolet, which stood gleaming in the evening sun, and waited for her to get in before closing it. The upholstery smelt brand new and Chris wondered what he did for a living to afford such luxury.

The restaurant was only a short drive away, and it was not long before Mark located a parking space and was once again opening the passenger door.

"I think I could get used to this," Chris told herself, trying to get out as gracefully as she could and wishing she had chosen a slightly longer dress.

As they walked through the door a waiter hurried over to them and Mark gave him his name, saying that he had booked a table in the alcove. After offering to take Chris's coat and showing them to the table, the waiter scuttled off to get menus.

Mark smiled at Chris, staring directly into her eyes. She felt herself begin to blush and averted her gaze in the general direction of the other diners.

"A friend recommended this restaurant to me," he said, "I hope the food is good. I don't really know many places around here. I apologise in advance in case it turns out to be awful."

He flashed a grin at her, just as the waiter returned with the menus and a wine list, reeling off the specials as if reciting a script. He was so fast that Chris had to ask him to repeat them, feeling embarrassed that her brain had decided to desert her.

"This is going to be a long night," she thought.

They placed their orders and Mark chose the wine. So much for Chris's resolve to stop drinking! The waiter retrieved their menus and disappeared towards the kitchen.

An awkward silence fell between them, which Chris felt obliged to break.

"This is very nice of you," she began, "but you really didn't need to go to this trouble, just over some spilt coffee, especially as it was *me* who spilt it on *you*. I hope you'll let me at least go halves with the bill."

He smiled patiently at her, as if humouring a child.

"Certainly not," he scolded her. "This is my treat. I meant what I said about wanting to get to know you and I can't think of a better way than to hold you hostage over dinner."

The waiter arrived with the wine, making a grand gesture of presenting the label to Mark and awaiting his acknowledgement that he had brought the correct one. After tasting it, Mark nodded and the waiter poured a glass for Chris before turning to fill the other glass. Chris watched Mark's easy charm and politeness with the waiter and once again began to speculate about him.

He picked up his glass and held it out towards her.

"Here's to you...and coffee," he said, waiting for her to clink her glass with his. After taking a sip, he put his glass down and once again held her gaze.

"OK, Christina Newman," he said dramatically, "tell me all about you. Where do you come from? What are your likes and dislikes? What makes you tick?"

Chris squirmed a little. This was exactly the sort of thing she hated – talking about herself. It made her feel uneasy. She took a deep breath and tried to look nonchalant.

"Well, I was brought up in Oxford – my parents still live there," she began. "My mother is a teacher and my dad is an art dealer. He has a small shop in town. I have a younger brother, who's at university."

She paused to fuel herself with another mouthful of wine. Mark was still gazing directly at her.

"I did a marketing course at Edinburgh University, where I got my degree. Shortly after that I came to London, where I did a few temporary jobs before I started working for Feldman & Son, as a personal assistant. That's about it really – what about you?"

Just at that moment the starters arrived, giving Mark the chance to evade her question.

"You said you worked for the son," he asked. "Simon Feldman wasn't it? What's he like? As I said, my dealings with the company only involved his father." Chris noted the evasion, but answered his question anyway.

"He's an easy guy to work for," she replied, "although he's a bit formal. He never calls me by my Christian name or enters into any casual conversation. It's always strictly business. He's very dedicated to the company and his job. He's not married and I don't think he's seeing anyone, not that I would know about that anyway."

She hesitated for a moment before saying, almost to herself, that she sometimes felt he was a bit lonely. Realising what she had said, she quickly turned her attention to the plate of food in front of her, taking a mouthful and trying to look casual.

"Umm," she exclaimed, hoping to change the subject, "this really is delicious."

He smiled at her, appearing to be relieved that she was enjoying the food.

Throughout the meal Mark continued to ask Chris about her job and the family who owned Feldman & Son, successfully managing to divert her attention away from him. He was quite keen to know about Simon's father, Daniel Feldman, but Chris did not know much about him, other than he lived somewhere in Esher.

While they were waiting for coffee, she decided he had evaded her questions long enough.

"I've told you all about me," she pointed out, "but I still don't know very much about you, so come on – spill!"

Mark could see that she was not going to let him off the hook, and thought carefully for a moment before answering.

"I'm quite a boring person really," he finally stated. "I spent most of my early years at boarding school, followed by three years at college. I tried my hand at a number of things, including a spell in the City, but didn't really enjoy any of them. Then, on my twenty-fifth birthday, a trust fund that had been set up for me by a wealthy relative matured and I suddenly found myself quite well off. Now I'm pretty much my own boss."

He paused and grinned. "Told you…boring!"

Chris was wide-eyed now.

"I don't call that boring," she replied. "Well, that explains the car. Must have been some investment! I could do with a relative like that.

What do you do with your time, now that you're...*self sufficient?*"

"What ever I feel like doing," he said, leaning back in his seat and throwing his hands in the air. "Right now I'm staying with a friend while I do some research."

The waiter arrived again with their coffees.

"How long will you be staying?" she asked, pouring some milk into her cup.

"I'm not sure," he replied. "Depends on my research."

He suddenly became lost in thought and started to drink his coffee. Chris tried a few times after that to get him to elaborate but he continued to be vague, saying that his stay in London was purely time out until he decided about his future plans. Eventually she gave up and excused herself, saying that she needed to visit the loo. As she left the table he summoned the waiter and asked for the bill.

As soon as he was sure that Chris was out of sight and the waiter occupied, he looked underneath the table for her bag, but she had taken it with her.

"Damn," he said under his breath. "It'll have to be plan B now."

He settled back into his chair just before the waiter returned with the bill. By the time Chris returned he had resumed a relaxed posture. He stood up, asked the waiter for Chris's coat and helped her on with it. Then, thanking the waiter, he escorted her out of the door, which was being held open for them.

They spent the journey back to Chris's flat in silence, both lost in their own thoughts. Chris did not like mysteries and Mark was enigmatic to say the least. But for all that, she still felt strangely relaxed in his company and found herself wanting to find out more about him.

When they reached Ebury Street, Mark again disregarded the yellow lines. He accompanied her through the entrance door to the flats, up the stairs and waited while she unlocked her front door.

Chris turned to look at him.

"Thank you for a nice evening," she said. "The meal was lovely. You can tell your friend it was an excellent choice." Hesitating she added: "Would you like to come in for another coffee before you go?"

Mark smiled softly at her.

"I'd love to, if I'm not pushing my luck," he replied, "although I'm afraid I can't stay too long. I have a full day ahead of me tomorrow. I promised I'd spend the day with my friend and his family. I think they're planning a picnic. I just hope it doesn't rain."

Chris laughed and ushered him in. She showed him into the lounge, throwing her coat onto the armchair as she passed. As he sat down on the sofa, Chris excused herself for a moment and went into the kitchen to make some coffee. While she was out of the room Mark got up and started to look around. He saw Chris's laptop on a small desk by the window. Looking cautiously over his shoulder to check that he was still alone, he opened the lid. It sprang into life, but unfortunately for Mark it had been logged out and needed a password.

"Damn it," he cursed for the second time that night.

He gently closed the lid and opened a notebook that was lying by the side of the laptop. He flipped through it quickly but found nothing that he considered useful, so he carefully put it back where he had found it. Hearing Chris coming back from the kitchen, he quickly returned to the sofa.

"OK, so it's going to be plan C," he thought.

CHAPTER 11

Chris spent all of Sunday trying to work out what exactly it was about Mark Dempster that made her feel both intrigued and uneasy.

He had been the perfect gentleman all evening – attentive, funny, not to mention 'dead hot', as Tessa had described him. In short, he was the sort of guy that usually only appeared in fantasy teenage romances and Barbara Cartland novels. The sort of guy, in fact, most young women dreamed of meeting, but rarely did.

However, something about him did not ring true. While they were having coffee she had asked him about his family, but he had simply said that, because of a disagreement with his mother and his stepfather, he did not have much contact with them these days. Apparently, they lived somewhere near the Kent coast. He had been reluctant to talk about them any more and had turned the conversation back to her. Shortly afterwards, he had finished his coffee, said he really had to go, wished her goodnight, given her a quick peck on the cheek and left.

He disappeared into the night, leaving Chris to realise that once again she had forgotten to get his telephone number. She had considered calling Tessa to chat about her apprehensions but thought better of it, in case she was with Peter.

Mark Dempster had also spent Sunday thinking. Saturday evening had not exactly turned out as planned. He had just meant to wine and dine the girl, turn on the charm and hopefully find out the precise whereabouts of Daniel Feldman. He had not expected to actually like her. However, when they had returned to her flat, and sat talking over coffee, he had found himself reluctantly warming to her. She had such an easy-going and natural personality that he had almost forgotten his original reason for coming back with her and had nearly given away too much.

Fortunately, he had left before completely forgetting his main objective. Unfortunately, in the cold light of day, here he was still thinking about her.

Now that she was clearly unable to provide him with any useful information, he had to put his feelings to one side and concentrate on Plan C – which was still in the planning stage. He needed to think – and fast!

CHAPTER 12

On Monday morning, Chris was sitting on the train to Sittingbourne, going over the notes on her laptop for the umpteenth time and trying to keep her mind focussed on what lay ahead. Today was important to her. It needed to be a success.

The 9.22 from London Victoria to Sittingbourne was going to take just over an hour, but after twenty minutes Chris had practically memorised all she needed to know about the company she so badly wanted to impress. She probably now knew more about them than they knew about themselves.

She closed her laptop and put it away in its case, then relaxed back in her seat and stared out of the window at the Kent countryside. The sun was not as bright today and hid behind the clouds. However, when the sun did appear it cast fleeting shadows across the fields and orchards.

Chris's mind gradually drifted back to her childhood. She had always enjoyed train journeys as a child. Her father had occasionally taken her with him on his buying trips to London. She had loved to look at all the different houses and gardens as they passed, imagining the lives of the people who lived inside. Other people's lives had always fascinated her. This thought led her back to Mark, and she wondered if she would get another chance to find out more about him. She was still wondering when the train pulled into Sittingbourne station.

At ten to eleven, Chris walked through the front entrance of Taylor-Wood and gave her name to the young girl at the reception desk – a girl who incidentally looked as if she had just left school. She soon found herself being shown into Colin Matthews' office. He looked younger than Chris had imagined from his voice, although there were grey flecks beginning to appear in his hair. He got up as she came in and Chris noted that he was quite tall and fairly slim, although a slight stomach bulge was visible beneath the pale blue shirt he was wearing under his unbuttoned grey jacket.

They shook hands while he asked her if she would like some coffee. As she had left the flat in her customary hurry, and had not had time for breakfast, she readily accepted. His secretary smiled, offered to take Chris's coat, and went to fetch the coffee.

"I must say, Miss Newman," he said, indicating for her to take a seat before sitting down himself, "I was quite intrigued after our conversation on Thursday. I've been looking forward to hearing how you think your company can be of benefit to us. I have to admit, I did some research of my own and it seems that Feldman & Son does indeed have a good reputation."

His secretary chose that moment to bring in the coffee, also placing a plate of biscuits on the desk alongside it. Chris eyed them discreetly, hoping that her stomach would not give away how hungry she felt.

"That's very reassuring to hear and I'm very grateful to you for giving me the opportunity to demonstrate how we can help you go international," she replied, reaching for her briefcase and extracting her laptop. She put it on the desk and opened the presentation.

"If you would care to take a look at the presentation we've prepared, it will give you a good idea of the services we can offer and the high standards we work to. It will also give you testimonials from some of our clients, although if you've visited our website you've probably already read them," she began, turning the laptop round and placing it on the desk, facing him.

"There are also some examples there of the marketing campaigns we've handled for them. You'll see that we have dealings with countries all over the world, each company with a diverse selection of products. Having offices worldwide means that we have access to numerous advertising and marketing contacts. Therefore, I feel confident that we can help you select the right market for your particular products. Please feel free to ask me any questions you may have."

She paused, took a sip of coffee and bit into a chocolate biscuit.

"I took the liberty of acquainting myself with your company's history and your product portfolio," she continued, feeling a little more confident now, as she watched him scan the presentation with interest. "Your scarves and ties are of the highest quality and reach a premium market. They are also in great demand here in the UK. Based on that, and our international market analysis, I feel that Italy would be a very good place to start promoting your merchandise."

She waited while Colin Matthews finished looking through the presentation, watching his expression and trying to gauge his thoughts as she answered his questions. He gave nothing away.

Finally, he smiled at her.

"Actually, Miss Newman, your timing is perfect," he said, handing the laptop back to her. "We've been thinking about whether or not we should try expanding abroad and only last week, at a board meeting, we decided that maybe we should give it serious consideration."

He leaned back in his chair.

"I need to consult with my colleagues," he continued, "as we will need to look into the various export requirements. But when that's done I'm sure we will also consider the marketing side of things. Your company would certainly be top of the list when we're ready to set things in motion. Do you have anything I can keep and show to my colleagues?"

Chris smiled. Obviously she had not made a complete idiot of herself.

"Yes," she replied, returning to her briefcase. "I can let you have a CD with the presentation on it or, if you prefer, a hard copy... or both."

"A CD will be fine. Thank you," he smiled, rising from his chair and taking the CD from Chris. He put the CD in his desk drawer and began to move around the desk towards her. She took that to mean that the meeting was over, and so, following his lead, put the laptop back in her case and got up.

"If you could leave your contact details with my secretary I'll get her to let you know when we've made our decision," he said.

"The details are all on the CD," Chris replied, "but if I may leave you my card, I'll also leave one with your secretary."

Colin Matthews took the card. They shook hands again, and thanking him she left his office in search of her coat.

On the train back to Victoria, she phoned the office to let Simon know how things had gone. He seemed impressed with her first solo meeting.

"First blood!" she thought to herself, and with a smile retrieved an i-pod from her bag, put the headphones in her ears and gazed contentedly out at the Garden of England.

CHAPTER 13

On Tuesday morning Chris was at her desk early. This could become a habit, she laughed, feeling quite proud of herself, having had an early night *and* actually woken up with her alarm. She had ignored the usual cheeky remarks from Tim when passing the reception desk, and the marketing team, who had apparently become bored with their own jokes, now merely returned her cheerful greeting.

Anyway, after her first potential triumph yesterday she was not going to let anything upset her euphoria.

When Simon Feldman arrived, he registered her presence with a reserved smile and asked her to come into his office. She grabbed her laptop, which contained the notes she had made from the meeting, and followed him in, waiting while he hung up his coat. As his secretary brought in his usual morning coffee, he waved Chris towards the chair in front of his desk and she sat down.

"Well Miss Newman," he said, controlling a smile and sitting down himself. "I believe congratulations are in order. It sounds as if you may have hooked your first client. My first encounter was a complete disaster, but then I wasn't as focussed as you back then. It took me some time to get to grips with my new career, so to speak. You, however, appear to be a natural. Tell me the details."

Chris felt a smug feeling of self-satisfaction well up inside her, but composed herself, opened her laptop and found her notes.

"Mr Matthews had done his homework, it seems," she said. "Fortunately what he'd found out was very much in our favour. The company's reputation had obviously preceded my arrival. It was also fortuitous that Taylor-Wood had already been thinking along the lines of moving into the international market. They just need to start investigating all the procedures and pitfalls of actually exporting their goods before they turn their attention to marketing strategy. He's going to contact me when they're ready to talk about our potential role, but he was very positive. I recommended Italy to him, at least to start with."

Simon smiled at her enthusiasm.

"Good," he replied. "You seem to have everything under control. Let's hope they follow through. In the meantime, if you are going to go down the Italian route, perhaps it's time you acquainted yourself with the people you'd be working with in Rome. I'm pretty much free after Wednesday, so I thought we'd catch a plane to Rome on Thursday morning, meet the guys at our Rome office, have dinner and come back on Friday morning. You don't have anything planned on those days do you?"

He was already checking his diary and making an entry.

"No, at least nothing that can't wait until the following week," she answered, trying not to sound too excited.

"Fine," Simon said, reaching for the telephone and dialling his secretary's internal number. "I'll get Mrs Summers to book the flights and accommodation. There's a hotel just around the corner from the office that we regularly use, in the Via Nazionale. The rooms are comfortable and it's convenient. You do have an up-to-date passport I presume?"

Chris confirmed that she had and went back to her office, grinning from ear to ear and trying to appear as if this was an everyday occurrence for her.

* * * * * *

Mark Dempster was sitting in a coffee house, just across the road from Feldman & Son, where he had a good view of the main door and of everyone who came and went through it.

It was close to lunchtime and he had spent most of the morning contemplating his next move. He was also finding it increasingly difficult to stop thinking about Chris, which was annoying him.

Over the last two years he had brooded on and off about Daniel Feldman, but his sudden wealth had caused him to be distracted by the pursuit of enjoyment that the money afforded him. It was only recently that he had decided to take things further and locate him. And now that he had let a woman enter his mind he was once again becoming distracted.

He forced himself to concentrate on the matter in hand. His new lifestyle had made him lazy, and he knew he was looking for the easiest way of getting to Feldman with the minimum of effort. He had thought about trying to get to know the secretary, but had dismissed the idea as a waste of time. According to Tim, she was married and a bit of a dragon. She had also worked for the Feldmans for many years and was fiercely loyal. He had made a few half-hearted attempts to trace him on the Internet but it had proved much trickier than expected and he had lacked the focus to see them through. The thought of befriending a young woman from the company had been much more to his liking, which was why he had chosen to home in on Chris.

He leant back in his chair and stretched lazily, his eyes casually following two mini-skirted girls who just happened to pass by the window. He smiled in appreciation of the view.

As he finished his third cup of coffee and placed the cup back on the saucer, he saw Chris come out of the building and make her way down the road, in the direction of the sandwich bar. He watched her until she disappeared from sight, then sat back in his seat and gave a quiet groan.

"Damn it!" he whispered to himself. Then taking his mobile out of his pocket he dialled a number and waited. A voice on the other end invited him to leave a message, which he duly did.

CHAPTER 14

Tuesday afternoon came and went, and Chris had tried again, and failed again, to reach the first two names on her list. With her newfound confidence and recent success, she was determined not to let anything prevent her from adding to it. So she felt immense pleasure when, re-contacting the third name, she managed to get an appointment for the following week.

Walking through the front door of her flat that evening she saw the message button on the telephone flashing and immediately thought of her mother.

"What now?" she said out loud, hanging up her coat and playing back the message. The voice she heard surprised her – it certainly was not her mother's.

"Hi Chris," she heard Mark say. "Just wanted to say how much I enjoyed Saturday. I wondered if you would like to repeat it sometime. Give me a call." He gave his mobile number and hung up.

Chris sat down by the phone with her hand to her mouth. She had mixed feelings about what she had just heard, as she had been unsure whether she would hear from him again. She had put Mark to the back of her mind, but now the niggling doubts resurfaced.

She went into the kitchen and took the solitary, almost empty bottle of white wine out of the fridge and drained it into a glass. Taking a large gulp, she went into the lounge and sat down on the sofa. She needed to think about this. Half of her told her to ignore and erase the message, but the other half was filled with overwhelming curiosity about why he was so evasive and secretive. At least she had a number for him now. Her curiosity won through and she went back into the hallway and dialled Mark's number.

She waited for him to answer. He did not keep her waiting long.

"Hi Mark, it's Chris," she said, trying to sound casual. "I got your message, thanks. It was quite unexpected but nice to hear from you. How are you?"

There was a brief pause at the other end, as if he was trying to gather his thoughts.

"I'm fine thanks," he eventually replied, apparently equally as casual. "I wasn't sure if you'd call back. I hoped you would, but I didn't want to presume in case I had completely blown my chances on Saturday and your experience of the evening had been totally different to mine." He gave a nervous laugh.

"It was a lovely evening Mark," she reassured him, "but I was convinced it was just a one off. You left without any indication that you wanted to repeat the encounter! However, I'm glad to hear that I was wrong."

There was another pause before he spoke.

"I would very much like to repeat it, if that's alright with you," he continued. "How about tomorrow night?" Chris decided to let him wait this time before answering.

"Tomorrow might not be a good idea. I'm going to Rome on business with Simon Feldman on Thursday and I'll need to be up early. I'll be back by the weekend though, so how about Saturday night?"

"Lucky you," he said, sounding a bit put out. "What a jet set life you lead. Saturday would be great. I'll pick you up around the same time – seven-thirty? See you then. Have a good trip. Bye." With that he abruptly hung up.

"Charming," Chris said to the dead line, and replaced the receiver.

* * * * * *

Mark smiled to himself as he hung up on Chris. Plan C had now formulated in his quick mind. He dialled another number.

"Rome, eh. That's a bit of luck. Both of them too," he thought as he waited for an answer to his call. He did not have long to wait before he heard the familiar voice answer.

"Got a little job for you tomorrow Timbo," he said, not bothering to waste time with pleasantries. "I gather your boss is out of the country for the next two days. Think you can gain access to his office at some point to do a spot of detective work? I know how resourceful you can be. You might need to blag your way past the secretary though."

The answer was obviously hesitant, because Mark's confident tone changed to one of irritation.

"Of course you can," he snapped. "Don't forget, I'm relying on you. See you later." He pushed the 'end call' button on his phone and put it back in his pocket.

CHAPTER 15

The day after Mark's phone call, Chris tried not to think about him, preferring to concentrate on her work. The excitement of her impending trip to Italy made that relatively easy.

On returning to her flat, she spent the evening packing a few overnight things before ringing Tessa to find out how her weekend had gone. Apparently it had gone very well indeed, if the fact that Peter had stayed over was anything to go by.

"You're unbelievable," Chris told her, rolling her eyes and laughing. "I bet the poor boy didn't know what had hit him! I don't know how you do it."

Tessa feigned indignation and adopted a hurt tone.

"I don't know what you mean, I'm sure," she replied, unable to stop herself giggling. "Seriously, though – he was certainly worth the effort," she continued. "How about your date? Did you have a good time? Did you have *breakfast* together?"

Chris just sighed.

"For Heaven's sake!" she exclaimed, tutting. "No we didn't. I had a nice evening though. He was charming, polite, attentive – but absolutely, infuriatingly tight-lipped about himself, apart from the bare necessities. He's got a great car though. I think he must be a bank robber – or a drugs dealer!" She paused for dramatic effect before continuing. "I'm seeing him again on Saturday night, after I get back from Rome. He's probably going to tell me he's a *spy*."

Tessa erupted into laughter.

"Really Chris, you're such a fantasist," she replied, still laughing. "He's probably something deadly boring and a bit shy. Still, it's nice to hear that you've finally joined the sisterhood and jumped into the sea of dating! I'll look forward to the second instalment."

* * * * * * *

At six-thirty on Thursday morning, Chris was sitting in the departure area at Heathrow Airport's Terminal 4, sleepy-eyed and waiting for Simon. They were booked on the seven-thirty Alitalia flight to Rome's Fiumicino Airport and she really needed a coffee! She had been up since four-thirty, terrified she was going to be late and miss the plane. She had arranged for a BT early morning alarm call to make sure she was ready for the taxi, and while she waited for it to arrive she concluded once and for all that she was definitely not a morning person.

The airport seemed busy for so early in the morning she thought, although not being a frequent flyer she was not really sure if this was normal or not.

She glanced at her watch and Simon appeared beside her. He took charge of getting the two of them through baggage check and passport control to the departure lounge. Finally, he asked if she would like a coffee.

"Yes, *please*," she gratefully replied.

While she waited for him to get the drinks, she sat down next to a woman with two excited children. The husband was trying hard to read a newspaper while they chattered incessantly. They were obviously off on holiday, Chris thought. The kids reminded her of her brother Adam, hyped up on the way to their family holidays in Spain. They were fond memories.

Simon returned with the coffee and made awkward small talk until the departure board announced that their flight was now boarding. At exactly seven-thirty they were in their seats listening to the flight information and safety procedures, demonstrated with exaggerated gestures by the cabin crew, while the plane taxied towards the runway. With a sudden roar of the engine, the plane accelerated and they were soon airborne and on their way to Rome.

It was a two-and-a-half hour flight, so Chris made herself comfortable in her seat by the window. While Simon became absorbed in his complimentary newspaper, she felt her eyelids grow heavy and drifted into a dreamless sleep. She awoke suddenly, hearing a voice asking her if she would like something to eat or drink. She accepted the breakfast that was being offered and asked for some coffee. The smiling stewardess readily obliged. She could get used to this Business Class travel, Chris thought to herself.

The plane landed at eleven o'clock local time and they were soon in a taxi, speeding towards the centre of Rome. Chris had never been to Italy before and she eagerly took in every second of the journey to the hotel. Once they had checked in Simon suggested that they should go to their rooms, freshen-up and meet in reception in about half-an-hour to go out to lunch. It was a glorious day and eating *al fresco* was a nice way to enjoy Rome, he told her. Chris was not going to disagree.

At twelve-thirty they emerged onto the Via Nazionale and walked across the road to a nearby taxi stand. They were in luck as there were two white taxis already waiting at the stand, and, unusually, there was no queue. Simon spoke to the driver in Italian as he opened the rear door for Chris to get in, before sliding into the seat beside her himself. The early afternoon sun was quite hot, despite the mild breeze, and Chris was grateful to feel the air conditioning inside the car.

The driver smiled at her through his rear view mirror. He was young, probably not much older than her, and obviously enjoyed flirting with his female passengers. Chris tried not to show her embarrassment and turned to look out of the window as he turned the taxi around and sped off.

She took in the sights and sounds, watching with interest the people bustling along to their various destinations. A group of young girls, clad in fashionable summer clothes, flirting with boys who wolf-whistled at them as they passed by; office workers enjoying the sunshine before going back to their desks; tourists consulting maps and pointing at things, while chattering away to each other in various languages – in short, it was a colourful, vibrant picture which filled

Chris with excitement. Her first time in Rome and already she knew she was going to love it.

The taxi pulled up outside a restaurant in Via Nicola Salvi. Simon paid the driver, thanked him and guided Chris towards the entrance. It was obviously a popular place as it was buzzing, inside and out.

"Would you like to sit outside?" he asked her, indicating the terrace. "It's mostly in the shade and, as you can see, has a great view of the Coliseum."

Chris looked to where he was pointing and took in the famous landmark. Today was just getting better, she thought.

"Outside it is then," she replied, as a waiter came over to them.

They followed him to a table and sat down. The waiter handed them menus and asked if he could get them a drink.

"If you don't mind," Chris said, looking at Simon, "I would just like a very cold orange juice. I've never been very good with the heat and if we are going to be working this afternoon I don't want to be falling asleep."

He laughed and, turning to the waiter, ordered a juice for her and a beer for himself.

"Have you been to Rome before?" he asked her, while looking at the menu.

Chris peered at him from over the top of hers, noting that he had barely glanced at his before putting it down and turning his attention to her.

"No," she replied. "And I had no idea it was going to be so stunning."

The waiter returned with their drinks and asked if they had chosen their food. Simon ordered a pasta dish and Chris asked for a Caesar salad. He took a sip of beer and smiled across the table at her. She had never seen him so relaxed.

"I always feel so at home here," he said, as if reading her mind.

Leaning back in his chair and drifting his gaze towards the view, he eventually returned his attention to Chris. This was a side to her boss that she had not seen before. She was not sure how to respond, so decided to keep it formal for the time being.

"I know from the others in the office that some of your family are from Italy, Mr Feldman," she began, "but I got the impression that they lived out in the country."

Simon rolled his eyes at her and chuckled to himself.

"I think I owe you an apology, Christina," he finally said. "I can see how formal I have been with you since you joined us, and I realise now just how strange that must have seemed to you. After all, you are supposed to be my right-hand man, so to speak. So please, call me Simon."

Chris was not quite sure what to say. His relaxed friendliness had taken her by surprise. It was the first time he had used her Christian name, so all she could manage to say was a feeble "OK!"

"You're quite right about my family," he continued, "although it was only my grandmother who was truly Italian. My grandfather was English and she met him after the war. She came from a small place called Monteriggioni, in Tuscany apparently. I only found that out myself last weekend. As a family, we have never found communication with each other that easy. That's probably why I tend to keep most people at arm's length – it requires less effort. I promise

I'll do my best not to be like that with you."

He grinned and Chris felt her tension begin to ease. The waiter arrived with their food and as they ate their lunch, she began to feel a little bolder.

"If you don't mind me asking," she ventured, scooping up a lettuce leaf with her fork, "why did your father retire early? I heard that it was due to illness."

She waited for his reply, hoping she had not spoken out of turn. The question did not seem to bother him.

"He developed emphysema," he said casually. "It's apparently in its early stages but he needs to take it easy. My mother thought that he was working too hard. She felt that it was about time he thought about his health, and the effect his disregard for it was having on the family, rather than spending all of his time wrapped up in expanding the Feldman Empire! That's where I came in."

He sighed, mulling the thought over in his head while twirling some pasta onto his fork.

"I really didn't want to take on the mantle," he admitted. "After university I had plans of my own. I'm an only child and I've always been a bit of a loner. I travelled around Europe for a year before my father summoned me home – he's not someone you say no to. Suddenly I found myself responsible for an army of people worldwide, all looking to me to come up with the goods – some of them easier to deal with than others, I might add!"

He uncharacteristically winked at her and Chris could not help laughing, almost choking on a crouton.

They continued their lunch in the same light-hearted vein,

exchanging background stories, likes and dislikes and gradually feeling more at ease with each other. So engrossed were they that they failed to notice the olive-skinned, young Italian man at the table behind them, who, having heard the names Feldman and Monteriggioni, was now hanging on their every word. He was dressed casually in faded jeans and a white T-shirt, and looked as if he had forgotten to shave that morning. The more he heard the darker his expression became.

When they had finished their lunch, Simon looked at his watch and summoned the waiter, asking for the bill. Chris admired the easy way he spoke Italian and decided that it sounded like a very romantic language.

"We'd better do some work now to justify this trip," he said, paying the bill on the waiter's return. "I told Antonio we'd be at the office in Via Firenza by about two-thirty, so we'd better get our skates on."

They left the restaurant and hailed another taxi. As they left the young man's eyes followed them burning with hatred as he pulled out his mobile phone.

Dialling a number he waited impatiently for it to be answered, before growling into it in Italian.

"What kept you?" he hissed, "God has finally rewarded our patience and this time Feldman won't escape his date with destiny. Meet me at the flat tonight, I have a little job for you."

He hung up and put the phone back into the pocket of his jeans. Then summoning the waiter, he paid his bill and left the restaurant.

CHAPTER 16

Back in London, Tim was trying to figure out how he was going to acquire the information Mark wanted. Chris and Simon might not be in their offices, but that dragon of a secretary was. He needed to distract her.

He leant back in his chair with his elbows on the arms, put his fingers together, rested them on his chin and tried to concentrate. Mark, with his obsession over Daniel Feldman's whereabouts, was fast becoming a pain. He wished that he had never allowed himself to be talked into helping him.

The morning passed slowly, bringing Tim no closer to a solution until, just before midday, fate took a hand. He found himself being addressed by Mrs Summers, who was standing in front of him at the reception desk, absent-mindedly adjusting her pinned up hair and looking flustered. She took him by surprise. She was not a naturally chatty person and rarely came down to reception.

"Timothy!" she barked at him, in a tone of voice that his old headmistress used whenever she had been annoyed with him. He bristled at the memory.

"I've just received a telephone call from my mother. She's had a slight fall and I need to go to her. It's unlikely that I'm going to make it back until the morning, so if there are any urgent phone calls while I'm away please take a message and tell them I'll get back to them as soon as possible. Should Mr Feldman call, please tell him what has happened and that I can be reached on my mobile in an emergency. He has the number."

She turned and swept out of the main door without waiting for Tim to reply.

Tim sat in shock for a while, unable to believe his luck. Someone up there was definitely on his side today. "No time like the present," he thought and reached under the counter to retrieve an engraved sign, which read:

'PLEASE TAKE A SEAT AND THE RECEPTIONIST WILL BE WITH YOU SHORTLY'

Placing it on the desk, he got up, scribbled a pretend note on a piece of paper, walked over to the lift and pressed the button.

On arrival at the first floor, he walked casually past the marketing team, smiling and returning their banter before heading up the corridor towards Simon's office. It was the first time he had been up here since his interview for the job. He still could not believe how easy this was turning out to be.

As he passed by the art department he could hear Brad Martinez's voice – he was telling the others a joke. Catching sight of Tim, Brad held his hand up in acknowledgement, then returned to his joke while the others burst into laughter. Things up here were definitely more relaxed when the boss was away, Tim thought.

He continued along the corridor with the piece of paper clutched firmly in his hand, in case anyone should ask what he was doing. He had rehearsed in his head the excuse of delivering a message, but by the time he reached Simon's office his presence had already been dismissed from everyone's thoughts. He was apparently deemed too unimportant to bother about. He gave a last look over his shoulder, to make sure that the dragon had not changed her mind, opened the door and went in. Because of its location at the end of the corridor the office was not readily in view, so he was able to snoop around unseen.

After checking the desktop and taking a quick look through Simon Feldman's desk diary, he opened the two drawers, one by one, carefully checking the contents so that it did not appear that they had been disturbed. Apart from the usual stationery, some loose receipts and a spare tie he found nothing of use. Feldman was certainly not a hoarder.

He pulled open the filing drawer and examined the assorted papers within the hanging files. Again he found nothing that would satisfy Mark. Simon's laptop was missing – he had obviously taken it with him.

Moving over to the bookshelves, he checked through the various files neatly stacked upon them. They were full of client records and correspondence, or various copies of invoices. No mention of Daniel Feldman.

Drawing a blank, he decided to try the secretary's desk next. He was sure that Chris would be less likely to have anything in her office concerning Daniel Feldman, but, if necessary, he would try there afterwards.

Slipping out of Simon's office and crossing over to the large alcove where his secretary sat, he ran his eyes over her desktop. Even in her haste, she had tided her desk and there was nothing obvious left lying around. He gently touched her computer mouse, but as the screen sprang to life he could see that it was logged out. He carefully searched her desk drawers instead. Still nothing! Silently cursing to himself, Tim finally crossed to Chris's office and gave it a cursory search. He was not surprised when that also proved fruitless.

He was just about to press the button for the lift when one of the women from finance saw him and came scuttling over.

"Ah, Tim," she exclaimed. "I'm glad I caught you. You've saved me a journey."

She was a middle-aged woman of about fifty, and had been with the company for almost as long as Elaine Summers.

"I know you haven't been with us for very long, but it's Mr and Mrs Feldman senior's wedding anniversary next week and I'm organising a collection for a nice bouquet of flowers from the staff. I wondered if you would like to contribute. They've always treated us so well that, even though Mr Feldman has retired, I thought it would be a nice gesture to show our appreciation. I can still remember those wonderful barbecues they used to hold for us in the summer."

She mused wistfully at the thought, giving Tim the opportunity to digest her words.

"You actually all went to Daniel Feldman's home," he asked in wide-eyed amazement.

Susan Bridger stared at him.

"Of course," she replied. "They have a large garden and used to hire a marquee with a band. I really miss those occasions. They even hired a minibus, so that everyone could have a drink. They were good times. Simon Feldman doesn't seem to have the same thoughtfulness as his father."

She sighed and held out the collection envelope to Tim, who felt obliged to rummage in his pocket. Pulling out a couple of pound coins, he placed them inside the envelope.

"Whereabouts do they live?" he asked casually.

Susan seemed eager to brag about her superior knowledge.

"They have a huge house in Esher," she told him with obvious satisfaction.

Tim realised that she was his best chance today, so he decided to massage her ego.

"That's interesting," he said encouragingly. "I have friends in Esher. I might have passed their house. Where exactly in Esher do they live?"

He was beginning to enjoy his subterfuge.

"I wouldn't have thought so, dear," retorted Susan. "It's a private road, just opposite the car park as you enter the High Street on the Portsmouth Road. Their house is the largest one at the end of the close. It's very secluded from the main road."

She smiled condescendingly at Tim. "As if he was likely to be in that league," she thought.

Tim agreed that he was indeed unaware of the property and

memorised the details she had given him, ignoring her insinuated insult. He had what he needed, so Tim pushed the button for the lift and watched Susan disappear into the art department, rattling her envelope.

"Good luck with that," he thought smiling.

CHAPTER 17

The taxi dropped Simon and Chris off outside the Feldman offices in the Via Firenza at just after two-thirty.

After paying the driver, Simon led Chris towards an entrance door by the side of a pizza restaurant. The building was nowhere near as grand as their office back in Mayfair, and had it not been for the nameplate on the wall, Chris would not have realised it was an office at all.

Simon rang the bell, announced his name when requested, and pushed open the door as soon as he heard the buzzer. They crossed the small, rather dingy lobby and climbed a flight of stairs to the first floor.

The office was surprisingly spacious, with two large windows overlooking the street. It also felt refreshingly cool, because of the air conditioning. By the windows were two desks, and a third stood by the door through which they had just entered. The walls had been painted white in an attempt to brighten the room, as the office was evidently often in shade from the buildings across the narrow street.

At the desks sat two men and a woman. The men were busy tapping away on their computers, while the woman conducted an animated conversation on the telephone in Italian. Simon introduced Chris to everyone individually before heading towards another door at the back of the room. Knocking, he waited for the invitation to enter, then opened the door and ushered Chris in.

This room was considerably smaller than the main reception area, but it too had a window overlooking the street. Its walls were also painted white. There was just one desk in here, behind which sat an Italian man of about forty, with dark, slightly greying hair and olive skin. As he saw them his brown eyes lit up and a broad smile spread across his face. Standing up, he walked around his desk and held out his hand to Simon.

"*Ciao*, Simon," he said shaking his hand. "Good to see you. How is your father? I hope he is resting as the doctor tells him."

After returning the pleasantries, Simon introduced Chris.

"This is Antonio Mancini, Christina. Antonio, this is Christina Newman, my assistant. She has a potential client who may be interested in making use of our services over here, so I thought it was about time you two got acquainted."

"Delighted to meet you at last, Christina," said Antonio, his smile widening further to display a set of white teeth that perfectly matched the walls. "I hope our little talk last week was of help and that we can work many times together."

Chris held out her hand to shake his, but he elaborately took hold of it and kissed the back of it. She gave him an embarrassed smile and tried to re-compose herself. It was going to take a while for her to get used to Italian charm.

"It's nice to finally meet you too, Antonio," she said, retrieving her hand as soon as she was able to do so without offending him.

Chris and Simon sat down on the two spare chairs in front of Antonio's desk, while he opened his door and asked for coffee and a jug of iced water.

"How long will you be staying in Rome, Simon?" he asked, retaking his seat. "We see so little of you here, although I suppose that also means you are happy with us. Your father used to come here a lot. He kept us on our toes. He worried about everything… I hope he has stopped worrying now. It is not good to fret too much."

There was a knock on the door, followed by the entrance of one of the men carrying a tray with three cups of coffee on it, together with a jug of water and three glasses. He put the tray down on the desk and disappeared back into the main office, closing the door behind him.

"We're only here until tomorrow morning, Antonio," replied Simon, taking a cup. "It's a flying visit really to give Christina a chance to get to know her Italian colleagues. It's always good to put a face to a voice. We're staying at the Palace Hotel around the corner. I thought I'd show Christina Rome by night. She can't go home without experiencing that."

He looked sideways at Chris and smiled. She found herself blushing slightly and tried to disguise it with a cough. Antonio laughed and poured her a glass of water, which she had requested instead of the coffee.

They stayed at the office until four o'clock, talking to everyone in turn. Chris asked questions about their roles and was shown a lot of material and photographs of various exhibitions and advertising campaigns they had organised. She found it immensely interesting and could not wait to get involved.

Looking at his watch, Simon suggested they should go back to the hotel, so that they could have some time to themselves before getting ready for dinner.

As they walked towards the Via Nazionale, discussing Chris's impressions of her Italian colleagues and the work they were doing, they were first watched from the shadows of a doorway, then followed at a safe distance.

On seeing them disappear through the hotel's entrance doors, the man stopped outside and made a mental note of the name of the hotel. He glared through the glass doors, turned and melted into the crowd of people bustling up and down the pavement.

CHAPTER 18

Chris sat in her room, drying her hair in front of the dressing table mirror. She had just had a relaxing soak in the bath and was now ready for the evening ahead.

It was still very warm, so when her hair was finally dry she put on a sleeveless, pale blue cotton dress and put her hair up to keep her face cool. She put on her make-up, then took out her flat evening sandals, which she had brought in case Simon planned to walk her round the city. She did not want to spoil her evening by nursing swollen feet!

At seven-thirty she grabbed her bag and a thin linen jacket and went down to the reception, where she sat on one of the large, comfortable sofas to wait for Simon. Before long, she saw him sauntering towards her, dressed in a pair of smart, light grey Chinos and a crisp white, short-sleeved shirt. He was carrying a pale blue linen jacket, which he had slung casually over his left shoulder. He looked very different from this afternoon when he had been wearing his business suit, and she had to remind herself that he was her boss.

"Ready to discover Rome?" he asked, smiling at her and offering her his hand to help her up.

"Absolutely, kind sir," she joked, following him out onto the street.

It was a lovely evening and Simon suggested that they should walk to the restaurant. Chris smiled to herself. "Right call with the shoes," she thought.

"It's only about a twenty minute walk," he reassured her, "but it will give you a feel for the city. It's a bar and restaurant that's a particular favourite with my father. He says it reminds him of Tuscany. He took me there the last time I came here with him. It's quite informal but the food is good."

She noticed the sense of anticipation in his voice.

They walked past bars and cafes, brimming with people enjoying the warmth of the summer evening. Conversation and laughter filled the air and Chris could not help but notice how many restaurants and bars had seating areas outside. She looked up at the various styles of the buildings they passed. Every now and then Simon would point out a particular piece of interesting architecture and tell her some of its history. He really seemed to love this city and it showed in his keenness for her to enjoy it too, like a little boy showing off his toys!

Eventually they arrived in the Via del Lavatore and Simon opened the door of the restaurant for Chris to enter. A hubbub of noise hit them as they walked inside. It was obviously a very popular place. A waiter rushed over to them and, very apologetically, said that all the outside tables were full but he could offer them one inside.

"That's fine," said Simon, and they followed him to a cosy table in the corner. The bar was decorated in shades of terracotta and all around the room were floor to ceiling shelves full of Chianti bottles. When the waiter brought the menus, Simon once again merely glanced at his and suggested that Chris try one of their pizzas.

"You won't be disappointed," he declared, smiling at her. "You can't come to Italy and not have a real Italian pizza."

Chris laughed and studied the list in front of her, deciding to go with the house pizza.

"Excellent choice," said Simon, "I'll have the same. I can recommend it. I can also recommend the Chianti, this place is famous for it. They have a large selection."

Chris knew he had already made up his mind which one he was going to order, so she nodded in agreement and let him take control.

As the meal progressed and they once again relaxed into each other's company, chatting freely about their lives and hopes for the business, Chris found herself comparing being with Simon to being with Mark. She had only spent a day getting to know Simon and already she knew far more about him than she felt she would ever know about Mark, who seemed to have gone out of his way to keep her at arm's length. Then she remembered what Mark had said about dealing with Daniel Feldman, so she decided to casually run it past Simon.

"Have you heard of a Mark Dempster?" she asked him, taking a sip of her wine.

Simon thought for a moment before replying.

"No, the name doesn't sound familiar," he replied, emptying the last of the wine into his glass. "Why?"

"It's just that I had dinner with a guy last Saturday," she said, "who claimed that he'd had dealings with your father. I just wondered if you knew what sort of dealings it might have been, as he wouldn't say and I got the distinct feeling that he's trying to hide something. Perhaps I'm being paranoid."

Simon stifled a laugh and raised an eyebrow.

"Sounds as if you've been reading too many detective stories, Christina," he said with a twinkle in his eye. "No man likes to give away all his secrets too soon, especially if he's trying to impress a girl. Do you like him?"

Chris felt herself blush.

"He's certainly got a lot of charm that's for sure, and I enjoyed his company," she continued, "but I just get this feeling that he's not entirely for real. Hot guys like him, suddenly and mysteriously wanting my company… well quite frankly, it just doesn't happen to me."

She sighed and drank some more wine. This time Simon could not contain the laughter.

"Good God, Christina," he cried. "You're not exactly a gorgon! Why shouldn't a good-looking guy, or any guy for that matter, want to hit on you? Are you seeing him again, if you don't mind me asking?"

Christina suddenly felt silly. Perhaps she was over-analysing the situation, but sharing her thoughts with someone else had made her all the more doubtful about Mark.

"I'm supposed to be seeing him on Saturday evening," she said, frowning. "Simon, I don't even know where he lives or what he does. He knows all about me though. Something just doesn't feel right, but

I can't help also feeling strangely attracted to him. Do you think I'm being silly?"

"I think we should get another bottle of wine and forget about Mark Dempster until you get back to London," he declared, looking around the room for a waiter. "Tonight we are in Rome and when in Rome, do as the Romans do… drink!"

Chris laughed as he finally managed to attract a waiter's attention and ordered more wine.

* * * * * * *

There was a cool breeze beginning to blow as they left the wine bar and Simon helped Chris on with her jacket before putting on his own. He suggested that they take a short detour on the way back to the hotel, as he wanted to show her the Trevi Fountain by night. Eagerly agreeing, she walked with him down the Via del Lavatore until they reached the Piazza di Trevi.

Chris gasped in astonishment when she saw the floodlit fountain in front of her. It was magnificent. The actual fountain adorned the side of a palatial building. It was in itself a work of art, with statues and columns surrounding a grand archway, inside which stood an imposing statue of Oceanus, the Greek Titan of all oceans and waterways. The whole edifice was illuminated in a glorious, yellowy-orange light, while the water of the fountain glowed a bright silvery blue, cascading over carved stones. Chris could not take her eyes off it.

Simon watched her face light up and smiled to himself with

satisfaction.

"You know, there is a legend which says that if you throw a coin into the fountain you will return to Rome again," he said, leaning on the outer wall of the fountain and staring into the water. "If you throw in two it will lead to a new romance, and three will secure you a marriage – or a divorce. Judging by what you told me over dinner, I'd stick to just the two if I were you!"

He turned towards Chris and winked. She clasped her hand to her chest and opened her mouth, feigning shock. He laughed and looked back towards the fountain, to savour its splendour. They stood there for a while, each lost in their own thoughts, until Simon broke the silence by asking her if she was ready to go back to the hotel.

Chris felt quite light-headed on the way back. She had definitely fallen under the spell of Rome, or was it just the wine? It was ten-thirty in the evening but everywhere was still teeming with people. It was so alive and exciting here. Going home to her quiet flat and her frozen meals was going to be such an anti-climax.

They reached the hotel and, once inside the reception area, Simon asked Chris if she would like a nightcap. She considered for a moment and then declined.

"I think I should go straight to bed," she said. "We both know the trouble I seem to have with being on time in the mornings, so it's probably better if I at least try to get a good night's sleep."

He laughed and, rolling his eyes, reluctantly agreed with her.

"I had Mrs Summers book a later flight back so that we could have a leisurely breakfast and drop into the office before leaving," he said. "I have one or two more things to discuss with Antonio before we head for the airport, so I'll see you in the breakfast room tomorrow morning at about eight-thirty. *Buona Notte* Christina."

Chris said goodnight and walked towards the lift. He watched her disappear inside before heading towards the bar.

CHAPTER 19

Simon was still on a high when he entered the hotel bar. He had looked forward to being back in Rome and was not quite ready for the day to end just yet.

Spending time with Chris had proved to be extremely enjoyable. He could not remember the last time he had felt able to talk so much about his life to anyone. It was quite liberating. He congratulated himself on choosing the right assistant and, now that he knew her better, he felt that he could maybe relax a little more around her.

In a way it was a pity she worked for him, as she was just the kind of girl he could have a proper relationship with. He had listened to his father's warning about personal liaisons with the staff and dismissed Chris from his mind. But he could not understand why his father had been so worked up about it. Surely he knew by now how transient his relationships seemed to be.

He sat down at the bar and ordered himself a brandy. The barman poured him a glass and as he picked it up, Simon cast his eye around the room for somewhere comfortable to savour his drink at leisure. As he did so, his eye fell upon a very attractive Italian woman, sitting at the end of the bar with an almost empty glass of red wine in front of her. She was dressed in an elegant black dress, which flattered her slim figure, and her dark hair fell softly around her shoulders. They were the only two people in the bar, and Simon surmised that she was on her own. On cue, she smiled at Simon and, feeling a little mellow from the Chianti he had consumed earlier, he decided to be bold and join her. She did not appear to mind as he sat on the stool beside her and asked if he could buy her a drink. She graciously accepted his offer and asked for another red wine.

"My name's Simon," he said, putting his glass down on the counter and offering her his hand. She laughed and gave him hers, saying in perfect English, with just a hint of an Italian accent, that her name was Adrianna. Simon kissed the back of her hand, Italian style, and picking up his glass again, raised it in a toast.

"To you, Adrianna," he said, "and beautiful women everywhere."

He took a sip and replaced the glass on the counter. Adrianna smiled at him enigmatically and took a sip from her glass.

"Bit of an old fashioned cliché," he slurred slightly, "but what is such a lovely woman like you doing on her own in a bar? Please don't tell me you're waiting for someone. I'll be mortified."

He put his hand on his heart and tried to look hurt. Adrianna laughed.

"I was supposed to be meeting a friend here," she said, "but it appears she has stood me up. I was just thinking of leaving."

Simon's eyes lit up. The brandy was now contributing to his

general feeling of intoxication.

"Then it's your friend's loss and my lucky night," he said, gazing into her brown eyes. "Let me make up for your disappointing evening so far. Stay and tell me all about yourself. The evening is still young."

Simon ordered another brandy and glass of red wine and they adjourned to a table in the corner, where they sat talking and laughing. Eventually, Adrianna stood up and said that she really ought to be going home. Simon stood up too.

"At least let me have your telephone number," he said with disappointment in his voice. "I'm returning to London tomorrow, but I have an office nearby so I could arrange to come back soon. I'd really like to see you again, Adrianna."

She smiled and taking a small diary from her bag, tore off a piece from the back and wrote her mobile number on it.

"You can have this only if you give me your number," she said, waving the paper tantalisingly in the air in front of him. "I have friends in London. You never know, I might surprise you one day."

She giggled while Simon desperately searched for something to write his number on, finally settling on a paper drinks coaster

They exchanged numbers and she kissed him gently on the cheek, before gliding out of the bar. Simon watched her go and sighed to himself. Yes, today had been extremely enjoyable. He suddenly felt very tired and, after tipping the barman, made his way slowly towards the lifts. He was going to sleep well tonight.

* * * * * *

117

Once outside, Adrianna checked to make sure she was not being followed and hurried around the corner to where she had parked her car. Unlocking the door and getting inside, she took her mobile out of her bag and dialled a number. It was answered almost immediately.

"Hi, it's me," she said in Italian. The man's voice on the other end sounded impatient, causing Adrianna to adopt a tone of annoyance. "Of course I got it," she snapped, clearly insulted by the suggestion that she could have failed.

"British men are all so predictable, especially when they're drunk," she continued. "They inexplicably feel irresistible to women. I merely had to indulge his illusions."

She looked out of the car window, anger flickering across her face.

"He's going back to England tomorrow, so, I think it's time for a little holiday in London."

She ended the call abruptly and threw the phone back into her bag before speeding off into the night.

CHAPTER 20

At seven-thirty the next morning Chris awoke to the sound of the telephone on the bedside cabinet ringing. Answering it, she heard the soft voice of the receptionist informing her of the time, just as she had requested the night before. Chris thanked her and replaced the receiver.

Leaning back on her elbows and rubbing the sleep from her eyes, she gazed around the room, getting her bearings. That Chianti had really been quite potent. She made her way to the bathroom and began the task of trying to transform herself into someone vaguely human, instead of the wreck she resembled.

By eight-thirty she felt fit enough to face the rest of the world, so she picked up her bag and key card, left the room and headed downstairs for breakfast. Simon was already there, sitting at a table with a large coffee in front of him.

"How can he look so fresh and awake after consuming just as much wine as I did last night," she wondered, walking over to him.

119

He got up, smiling at her.

"Good morning Christina," he said cheerfully. "I hope you managed to sleep well. It was a great evening, I really must come back here more often. I hope you enjoyed the sights, although, I have to say, you're looking slightly jaded."

He chuckled and pulled a chair out for her to sit on. She groaned at him and sat down.

"I got the receptionist to call me," she replied, "so you can thank her that you're not still waiting for me."

They shared a leisurely breakfast and returned to their rooms to collect their luggage. Simon of course needed to have his meeting with Antonio, so Chris decided to make good use of the time by discussing the possible marketing opportunities that she could offer Taylor-Wood. If she managed to secure the contract it would be Antonio's assistant, Carla Moretti, who would be her main contact, so she had a good chat with Carla. She handled all the exhibition work, passing any advertising that was required on to her colleagues.

Chris knew straight away that she was going to enjoy working with Carla. She was a bit older than Chris and, as the only female in the office, had quickly learnt to be more than a match for the others, but without losing her softer side. She was obviously kind-hearted and intelligent, and Chris saw she could learn a lot from her.

They left the office in good time to make it to the airport, and by one-thirty they were seated on the aeroplane, taking off for Heathrow.

Chris felt a tinge of regret leaving Rome. She had seen a different side to Simon away from the London office, and now that they were returning to normality she wondered if he would revert to his usual distant self. She hoped not – she quite liked this relaxed Simon.

As they flew over the city, Chris took a last look at the sprawling array of ancient ruins nestling amongst the Roman landscape and hoped she would return soon. After all, she had thrown a single coin into the Trevi fountain.

CHAPTER 21

At three-thirty on Friday afternoon, as Chris was landing at Heathrow, Mark sat in his car with Tim, across the road from Daniel Feldman's house.

As soon as Tim had given him the address, Mark had insisted on driving down to check out the location for himself. However, now that he had finally found what he had been searching for for so long, he was not quite sure what to do next.

"Are we going to sit here indefinitely," moaned Tim "or do you actually have a plan? I do have a life you know!"

Mark ignored his comment and carried on studying the house. Typically ostentatious, he thought disdainfully before starting the engine and turning the car around.

"Where are we going?" asked Tim, looking confused. "I don't understand. Do you mean to tell me that, after going through all the hassle of getting that bloody address, and then taking time off work to drive all the way down here with you, you're just going to turn around and drive all the way back to London? You're crazy! Remind me to have you certified."

He slumped back in the passenger seat, turning his attention to the countryside, which was by now whizzing past them as Mark angrily hammered the accelerator. He always drove fast when he was angry.

"I'm not ready yet," he said, staring intently at the road ahead. "I need more time to decide what I'm going to do. I've been thinking about this moment ever since I found out about Daniel Feldman and his sordid deal. I don't want to give him any opportunity to wriggle out of facing up to what he's done. After all this time he can wait a bit longer. At least I know where to find him now."

Tim turned his gaze to Mark, observing the dark frown that enveloped his face. "The sooner this is all over the better, before it gets out of hand," he thought.

Once back in London, Mark dropped Tim off in town and drove back to the flat they shared. As soon as he had discovered that Tim had got the job at Feldman & Son, he had asked him to put him up for a few weeks. That was, of course, before he had explained his plan. The more Tim knew, the more Mark regretted involving him. It really was not his problem. He did not want him to risk his job because of it, but he needed backup and Tim was the only person he trusted.

Opening the front door of the flat, Mark threw his car keys onto the small table that was just inside and headed for the lounge, where he slumped onto the sofa and kicked off his shoes. After letting his thoughts wander for a moment, he went into the kitchen, flung open the refrigerator and extracted a cold beer. Searching through one of the kitchen drawers, he found a bottle opener and prized off the top, taking a long swig from the bottle. It was a warm day and the cool liquid slid down a treat. Taking it with him back to the lounge, he put on a CD and slumped down on the sofa again.

He covered his eyes with his hand and let his mind drift, as the music filled the air around him. It was going to be a long evening and he had some serious thinking to do.

CHAPTER 22

On Saturday morning Chris awoke feeling relaxed and refreshed. After getting home the day before, she had unpacked, listened to her phone messages and then, sensibly, decided to have an early night. With all the excitement of Rome she had forgotten how tired she actually was, and the reality of being home had made her very aware of that fact.

Now she felt ready to face the weekend, but once out of bed and in the bathroom she began to ponder her date with Mark that evening. She had resolved to press him for some answers and began to plan in her head what she was going to say.

Things were going to be different tonight. She felt more in charge of the situation.

At barely seven-thirty the doorbell rang. Chris gave her hair a final check as she passed the hall mirror before opening the front door. Mark was leaning against the frame, grinning. This time he was dressed more casually – in a pair of smart black cord trousers with a red and white checked shirt. He still looked great, but something told Chris that tonight was going to be far less formal than last Saturday. She was glad that she had opted for a more understated look herself. Also, there were no flowers. He obviously no longer felt the need to impress her.

The air was still warm when they emerged into the street. She noted with a wry smile that the car was again parked in blatant contempt of the law, but this time the roof was down. Once in the car, he turned to her and gave her the same enigmatic smile that had melted her last time.

"I thought that, as it's such a warm evening, we'd go for a stroll by the river before eating," he said, looking straight into her eyes. "I haven't booked anything specific, so we can decide where to eat later. The good thing about London is there's always a choice."

Chris nodded in agreement as he turned the ignition and drove off towards the Embankment.

He parked as close as he could to the South Bank and they were soon walking past the National Theatre towards Royal Festival Hall. The area was full of people soaking up the atmosphere. Mime artists and human statues were performing their acts anywhere that offered enough space to attract a crowd. Chris loved this part of the river. It was always so alive.

As they strolled along, Mark casually reached out and took her hand in his. It surprised her for a moment, but she quite liked the easy familiarity with which he had done it. They stopped for a while to watch a pleasure boat gliding up the Thames, vibrant with the sound of laughter and music. He turned to smile at her and Chris hoped that tonight she would be able to get closer to him and find out what made him tick.

Eventually, a light, but cool breeze started to blow and Mark helped Chris on with the linen jacket she had been carrying. He suggested that they should perhaps find somewhere to eat. As a lot of the restaurants were already heaving with people, they settled on a Japanese restaurant, close to Festival Hall. It was not quite as busy as the other more popular family restaurants, and as it was a long time since she had had sushi, a hungry Chris read the menu excitedly.

After ordering, she sat back and decided the time was right to try once more to break through Mark's defences. He seemed quite relaxed.

"OK, Mark Dempster," she said with calm authority. "Tonight I'm not going to let you off so lightly. There's still a lot I don't know about you and I can't help getting the feeling that you're keeping something from me."

He was taken aback briefly, but the familiar guard was perceptibly raised as he put on an indulgent smile.

"I think you're letting your imagination run away with you, Chris," he said patiently. "I told you last week, my life is not that interesting. What more can I possibly tell you?"

Chris was not going to let him get away with that.

"OK, then," she continued. "Where are you living? What do you do with yourself all day? I know you said that you have access to enough money to do as you please, but what is that exactly?"

She felt she was on a roll but, just as she was about to press further, their food arrived, giving Mark a chance to gather his wits.

"I told you," he replied with a sigh. "I'm staying with a friend, while I decide what I want to do next. There really is no mystery about it Chris."

He dropped his gaze to his plate and began to eat. Chris bristled with annoyance and continued with her inquisition.

"That's not an answer Mark," she replied sharply. "You can't possibly be just sitting in a flat all day thinking. You must go out. Where do you go when you go out? And what happened that was so dreadful that you felt the need to break away from your parents? Where do they live anyway?"

Chris took a mouthful of food, but as she was now starting to feel that he was insulting her intelligence, her appetite had swiftly dwindled.

Mark, too, was beginning to feel annoyed. He was under attack and he did not like it. Why could she not just accept what he told her and leave it at that? Why did she have to spoil a perfectly nice evening? Was it not enough that he wanted her company?

"My relationship with my parents is my business, Chris," he snapped back. "It's nothing to do with you. I'll sort it out in my own good time, so please, can we drop it now and just enjoy the evening? I've been looking forward to seeing you tonight. Please don't spoil it."

His eyes were ablaze and Chris stared at him in amazement. She really resented his tone and behaviour and could no longer contain her anger. Throwing her napkin down onto the table, she jumped up, snatched her bag and jacket from the back of her chair and marched out of the restaurant.

"Where are you going?" he shouted after her. "Don't be so stupid. Come back."

Ignoring his protestations, Chris ran down the steps to the main road with tears of anger streaming down her face and looked desperately around for a taxi. She heard him behind her, shouting to her from the top of the steps, but when a black cab pulled up, she barked her address at the driver and jumped in, slamming the door and sinking into the seat. Trying to fight back the tears, she wished that she had never agreed to see Mark again. He could go to hell for all she cared.

* * * * * *

Mark stood in stunned silence at the top of the steps, watching Chris get into the taxi and disappear up the road. He could not believe what had just happened, particularly Chris's outburst. The women he normally went out with were only ever interested in having a good time, which suited him perfectly. They rarely asked him any questions about himself. This was a bit of a blow to his ego.

As he trudged back to his car, it slowly dawned on him. Chris was not like the other girls he had fleetingly known and, for that reason, he was beginning to care more about her than he had realised. But, however much he liked her, there was no way he could let her know his real motives for being in London… at least not yet.

CHAPTER 23

Chris paid the taxi driver and hurried into the lobby of the flats, wiping away the last of her tears as she went. She rushed up the stairs to her flat, opened the front door and banged it shut behind her. She leant backwards against the closed door and felt the tears start to flow again. Attempting to rub them away with her sleeve, she tossed her bag onto the floor, ran into the lounge and threw herself onto the sofa, where she lay staring vacantly across the room. Then, sitting up, she went over the events of the evening in her head and tried to make sense of it all. It had started out so well, strolling by the riverside. He had been so tender and then suddenly he had turned into a different person – one she did not recognise at all. For some reason, he scared her. Who was he?

She sat there for a while composing herself, then got up, took off her jacket and threw it down onto the sofa. She picked up the phone and dialled Tessa's number, sitting down on the chair beside the hall table.

After a while Tessa answered and she heard a man's voice in the background ask her who it was. "God, she must be with Peter," Chris thought and immediately regretted her call.

"Sorry Tessa," she apologised. "Bad timing? I'll call you back tomorrow." There was a sigh on the other end of the line.

"Don't be silly, sweetie," Tessa replied. "What on earth's the matter? You sound terrible. It's only Peter here and he won't mind. We've just ordered a pizza and it hasn't arrived yet so take your time and tell me what's happened."

Chris felt the tears well up again as she listened to her best friend's comforting voice. Sobbing, she related to Tessa everything that had happened, stopping occasionally to draw breath and wipe her nose. Tessa did not interrupt her, letting her pour everything out before she ventured an opinion.

"What a jerk," she snapped. "I could punch him for treating you like that. Who does he think he is? You don't need him, sweetie. A girl likes a bit of mystery now and again but that's just downright rude! Do you want to come over and get drunk with Pete and me tonight? We can order another pizza."

Chris had stopped crying now and was cheered by Tessa's outburst in her defence. She was such a good friend.

"No, thank you," she said, trying to laugh. "I feel much better now I've spoken to you. I don't know why I'm so surprised. I don't exactly have a great track record where men are concerned. No reason to expect things to change now. It's just that I was so hoping that Mark was going to be different, and that my misgivings were misplaced. I should have gone with my initial instinct that he was too good to be true. You have a nice evening with Pete. At least one of us seems to have the knack."

Tessa advised Chris to pour herself a large glass of wine and have a long soak in a hot bath. No man was worth that amount of aggravation, she announced. Chris promised she would follow those instructions. Then, replacing the receiver, she went into the kitchen to get the all-important wine, which thankfully she had bought earlier that day, before heading in the direction of the bathroom and bubbles.

CHAPTER 24

Simon had enjoyed a far less traumatic weekend than Chris. By the time he returned to his flat in Ennismore Gardens on Friday afternoon he had been feeling more like his old carefree self, and waking up on Saturday morning in his luxurious bedroom, with the sun streaming through the window, his positive outlook was reinforced.

In this frame of mind, he decided to invite some old university friends over for drinks in the evening. Being an all male gathering, the evening had quickly developed into a drinking contest and bun fight. So most of Sunday was spent getting rid of all the empty beer cans and wine bottles, as well as food debris, before his cleaner made an appearance the following day.

His flat was well suited for entertaining, situated in an elegant, leafy square opposite a private garden, in Knightsbridge. It had a large lounge with three floor-to-ceiling French windows, all of which led onto a balcony overlooking the square. The flat was owned by the company and had been used by his grandfather, followed by his father, to entertain important clients… and special friends. When Simon had joined the company his father had suggested he use it until he needed a more family-friendly residence. Daniel Feldman lived in hope of continuing the family empire. Unfortunately, Simon was still very fond of his bachelor status and showing no signs of relinquishing it.

It was now Monday morning and he was in his office reading his post. Chris was already at her desk when he arrived, but she did not seem like her usual cheerful self when he wished her good morning. He hoped it was nothing he had done, although that was unlikely, as he had not seen her since Friday and she had appeared fine then. "Still, you can never tell with women," he thought to himself.

After receiving his usual morning coffee from Mrs Summers and checking through his emails, he knocked on the glass partition between their offices and gestured Chris to come in. She gave a half smile, grabbed her laptop and joined him in his office.

"How are things going, Christina?" he asked casually, making a determined effort to be less formal with her. "Have you heard anything from Matthews at Taylor-Wood yet? How about your other contacts, any progress with them?"

Chris had not heard from Colin Matthews, but said she felt that it was too soon to expect a decision from him yet. He had explained to her there were quite a few things to sort out first, which would probably take him at least a couple of weeks.

"If I haven't heard from him by the end of the week," she said, consulting her laptop and typing in a reminder, "I'll phone him for a courtesy update. As for the other companies I contacted, I still couldn't get to speak to the first two on my list, but having spoken to the third I now have a meeting scheduled with the marketing director for tomorrow morning. Apparently they already have an outlet for their products in Germany, but they aren't happy with the way their current marketing associates are representing them and are keen to find out how we might be able to offer them a better service."

Simon watched her as she worked her way through her notes. There was definitely something else on her mind, he thought, but decided that it was none of his business as long as it did not interfere with her work. Still, he did not like to think that she was unhappy.

"Are you OK, Christina?" he finally ventured. "You seem preoccupied. Is there anything I can do? Are you worried about tomorrow?"

Christina, aware that she had let her personal feelings encroach on her working day, immediately changed the expression on her face to one of a happy, in-control professional. It was no mean feat, the way she was feeling this morning!

"Not at all," she replied, smiling at him. "I just had a disappointing weekend, that's all. After last week's trip to Rome, coming home was a bit of an anti-climax. However, I'm on track now, and ready to get down to business."

Simon relaxed, grateful that she was obviously not going to subject him to an emotional ordeal. He had never known what to do in those circumstances, so he sighed with relief and asked her to keep him in the loop. She assured him that she would and went back to her office. He then spent the rest of the morning catching up with paperwork and setting a few wheels in motion for his own most recent client.

* * * * * *

For Simon, the next two days passed in relative normality. On Tuesday, his mother phoned to ask if he could have another word with Daniel about the holiday in Italy, which she had proposed the last time Simon had visited them. He assured her that if, and when his father felt like travelling abroad, it would not be because of anything he had to say. His mother had huffed and made a comment about how the two of them were too much alike.

On the Wednesday, Chris had bound into his office, more like her usual self, and told him how successful her Tuesday meeting had been.

"In fact," she explained, "the company has just phoned and asked me to submit a campaign proposal with a breakdown of costs. Taylor-Wood also got in touch and asked me to do the same for them. Could we fix up a meeting to go over the details? I'd appreciate some guidance as it's my first time."

She was ecstatic, feeling she had finally made her mark. Simon was really pleased for her, knowing how hard she had worked, and promised he would make some time for her that afternoon.

By Thursday he had all but put the trip to Rome out of his mind, so when his mobile rang and the voice on the other end told him that it was Adrianna, it took him a few moments to recall who she was. He had, after all, consumed quite a bit of alcohol at the time.

"Of course," he said slowly, the memory gradually filtering back into his mind. "I didn't expect to hear from you. Women usually indulge me and then forget about me as soon as possible when I've been drinking. Apparently, I turn into an idiot."

She laughed, and hearing the familiar sound, Simon could now recall exactly how good Adrianna had looked that night.

"I hope you don't mind me calling," she continued, in her soft Italian accent, "but I'm in London for a few days, visiting the friends I told you about, and I wondered if you would like to meet up for a drink. You did ask for my number, but as I haven't heard from you, and this is the twenty-first century, I thought *I* would phone *you*."

Simon felt a flutter of excitement. It had been a while since he had dated anyone and the prospect of female company was very appealing.

"I'm glad you did. It's really good to hear from you, Adrianna," he replied. "How about tonight? Can you get to the Berkeley Hotel in Knightsbridge? I could meet you in the Blue Bar at about seven o'clock, if that's OK."

She told him that was fine and that she would see him later. She then hung up. He sat back in his chair and sighed with satisfaction, hoping that he had not sounded too keen. He did not want to frighten her off by appearing desperate.

By the time five o'clock arrived he felt like a schoolboy about to go on his very first date. Although it had been a while, he was no stranger to dating women. But this time it felt different. Tidying his desk and putting on his jacket, he waved goodnight to Chris and left the office to go back to his flat. Once there, he had a shower and changed into some smart, casual clothes. He dabbed his face with his favourite aftershave, combed his hair and checked the finished result in the full-length mirror in the hallway. Satisfied with his reflection, he smiled at himself and left the flat.

He arrived at the hotel bar early, not wanting to leave Adrianna waiting for him on her own, at the mercy of lounge lizards. Punctuality was something that his father had gone to great lengths to instil in him, saying that it always made a good impression and would serve him well in life. He always tried to follow that advice. He positioned himself at the bar and ordered a glass of whisky, keeping his eyes firmly on the door as he waited for the barman to pour it.

At just after seven, Adrianna glided gracefully into the Blue Bar, looking even more beautiful than the last time he had seen her. She was wearing a low-cut, midnight blue dress, just short enough to show off her long slender legs, with a black velvet jacket and black high-heels to complete the look. Her long, dark hair was piled up stylishly on top of her head. Simon felt the breath momentarily sucked out of his body. She walked straight over to where he stood at the bar and offered him her hand, which he held and raised to his lips, kissing it gently.

"You look amazing," Simon exclaimed, gazing into her eyes. "What would you like to drink?"

Apparently delighted at his reaction, she slid off her jacket and laid it on the bar stool beside her before sitting down on another and carefully crossing her elegant legs.

Simon ordered her a glass of red wine.

"To you," she said, raising her glass towards Simon before taking a sip. Her eyes held his gaze.

"To us," replied Simon, doing the same.

They sat talking and drinking for over an hour, during which time Simon decided that he definitely wanted to spend the entire evening with her. He asked if she was hungry and suggested that they eat at the hotel, as it was convenient, and they could continue their conversation. She agreed, and together they left the bar and made their way to the hotel's prestigious restaurant.

It was quite busy but Simon managed to get them an intimate table for two. He spent the whole meal gazing into Adrianna's eyes, absentmindedly placing food into his mouth from time to time while she asked him questions about his family and the company. He was so bewitched that he failed to register just how much information she was extracting from him and willingly told her everything she asked.

By the end of the meal it still felt relatively early, prompting Simon to ask Adrianna if she would like to come back to his flat for coffee, as he lived nearby. She could get a cab back from there. She agreed, and Simon felt a wave of excitement as he opened his front door and stepped back to let Adrianna enter the hallway.

He led her towards the lounge where she looked around with approval, noting the expensive furniture. Walking over to the French windows, she opened one and stepped onto the balcony.

"You have a wonderful view from here, even at night," she said, looking out across the square at the gardens, which were now lit by the street lights, before turning back to face Simon.

He crossed the room to join her, taking her in his arms and kissing her neck.

"Not as good as the view I have in here," he whispered into her ear, moving his lips to hers and kissing her softly but firmly.

She kissed him back and then gently pushed him away.

"Why don't you show me the rest of your flat," she purred, running a finger down his chest.

Simon released her, laughing.

"OK," he agreed, "but apart from the bathroom and kitchen, there's only the bedroom. So why don't we start there."

He took her hand and led her back into the hallway and through into the bedroom.

Adrianna gazed around the room slowly and turned to look at him seductively. She raised her hand to her hair and took out the pin, letting her soft dark tresses tumble around her shoulders. Reaching for the zip at the back of her dress, she undid it slowly and let the dress fall to the ground, revealing lacy black underwear.

She slid her arms around his neck.

"I think we can skip the bathroom and kitchen," she whispered, pulling him towards the bed. Simon felt the adrenalin rush through his body as she unbuttoned his shirt and lured him onto the bed. She was not going to need that taxi for a while.

* * * * * *

It was well past midnight by the time Adrianna returned to the rented flat in Battersea. She was tired, irritable and felt in urgent need of a shower to remove all traces of Simon. The thought of having been with him made her stomach churn.

She went into her bedroom and threw her bag onto the chair by the bed. She was aware of a presence behind her. Turning around she saw the Italian leaning against the doorframe with his arms folded. He had been waiting for her.

"At last," he said impatiently, "I've been freezing to death in this hell hole. What kept you? He's English... it couldn't have lasted that long!"

Adrianna ignored his sarcastic comments and sat down on the bed, shaking her shoes off onto the floor where they fell with a clatter.

"I had to make it look convincing," she replied, with more than a hint of annoyance in her voice. "You know how reserved the English can be. I didn't want it to look too obvious and make him suspicious. Anyway, I found out what we needed to know. Like candy from a baby, as the English say. You should be congratulating me, not whining! Now, if you don't mind I want to take a shower. I feel dirty! Please don't make me to do that again."

He watched her get up, slip off her dress and make her way to the bathroom, then heard the sound of running water as she switched on the shower.

"It was the only way to find out what we needed to know," he said. "Now we can finish what we came here to do and get back to Rome. The sooner the better in my opinion."

He looked around at the damp walls of the flat and grimaced. They had arrived that morning on an early flight and he was feeling cold and miserable. The temperature in Rome had been in the mid thirties when they left – unusually high for late August – but it was considerably cooler on landing at Heathrow, and even looked as if it might rain. He hated England. To him its people were as miserable as their weather. This bloody flat did nothing to lift his gloom either, but at least it was cheap.

He lingered for a while in the hallway, listening to the sound of the water cascading in the shower, then wandered into the lounge and turned on the battered old television that had been supplied with the flat. It sprang into life but the picture was fuzzy, so he jiggled the aerial and tried to adjust it. Settling for the best image he could get, he slumped down in a lumpy old armchair and tried to concentrate on the film that was showing, squirming to try to get even vaguely comfortable. Yes, he thought, the sooner the better.

CHAPTER 25

Simon woke up on the Friday morning still glowing with the memory of his evening with Adrianna.

For a moment he was not sure whether he had been dreaming about her, but the reality soon flooded back. The features of his bedroom came into focus and the events of last night formulated in his brain. Rubbing his eyes and casting his mind back, he was now certain that it had been real. He stretched out leisurely, running his hand down the side of the bed that she had been laying on only a few hours earlier. He could still smell her perfume lingering in the room.

He lay there for a while, savouring the memory of her body in his arms, before looking at his bedside clock and realising, with a start, that he was late. It was gone eight o'clock and he had slept through his alarm.

Jumping out of bed he hurried into the bathroom and ran the shower, singing contentedly to himself as the water revived him. Christina would find this lapse in his punctuality highly amusing, he thought as he lathered himself. Still, he was the boss and entitled to be late occasionally.

He dressed quickly, and then grabbed some toast and a mug of coffee before heading to the office. It was going to be a slow day after last night. He could not believe that such a beautiful girl could fall so easily into his lap. He decided he would ring her that morning and arrange to see her again, before she disappeared back to Italy.

Walking down the office corridor, he glanced into Chris's office and, seeing her already at her desk, gave her a cheery smile and wished her good morning. She smiled back, glancing at the clock on her wall and raising her eyebrows in amusement. He laughed and disappeared into his own office, asking Mrs Summers for his morning coffee as he went. Checking his post, he consulted his diary, saw he had no meetings scheduled and then phoned the mobile number that Adrianna had given him in Rome.

A sleepy voice answered.

"*Ciao, parlare di Adrianna,*" the voice said in what to Simon resembled a dream-like tone. He smiled to himself at the sound, so sexy even though she was barely awake.

"*Ciao, bella,*" he replied. She hesitated for a moment and then, recognising his voice, snapped into her role from the previous night. He had taken her by surprise but now she regained control of the situation.

"Simon," she purred, "How lovely to hear your voice, but I only left you a few hours ago. Are you missing me already?"

She laughed and Simon felt an over-whelming urge to be with her.

"Of course I am," he answered. "Last night was wonderful. I didn't want you to go and I missed you when I woke up this morning. When can I see you again, Adrianna? How about tonight?"

Again there was a moment's silence before she answered.

"I would love to see you Simon, but I must give some time to my friends. After all, I am staying with them," she lied.

The panic, however, was rising within her. She wanted nothing to do with him, but she could not risk arousing his suspicion. She had no choice but to agree to see him again. Her heart sank.

"How about next week? I will be in London for a week or two, so there will be time to see you again before I return to Rome," she continued, hoping that her voice did not betray the distaste she felt.

She need not have worried. Simon was well and truly under her spell and readily agreed to phone her on Monday to arrange somewhere to meet. On a high, he reluctantly said goodbye and hung up. Not only was today going to drag, but also the weekend.

* * * * * *

Adrianna jumped out of bed. She threw on a pair of jeans and a T-shirt and dashed down the hallway to her companion's room. She threw open the door and, rushing over to the bed, started to shake him. Rubbing his eyes, he sat up and yawned.

"I've just had a phone call from Simon Feldman, wanting to meet up again," she screamed at him. "I had no choice but to tell him that I'd see him again on Monday and I'm really not happy about that. Have you decided what we are going to do next? I can't pretend with him much longer."

He thoughtfully ran his fingers through his dishevelled hair, and then, throwing himself back onto his pillow, closed his eyes.

"It's early, Adrianna, *cara*," he moaned. "We have the whole weekend to think about this. Simon Feldman is not my main concern and I'm sure you can deal with him all by yourself. He doesn't seem to be able to resist your charms. He'll do whatever you ask him to do, so come back later and let me sleep."

Adrianna gave a cry of frustration and slapped him on his arm, almost propelling him out of the bed. She was angry now.

"The sooner you complete what we came here for the better," she shouted. "Do you actually have a plan? Get up and start thinking. I'm the one who's been doing all the work so far. It's your turn now."

She was pacing the room. He sat upright again and stared back at her, his eyes blazing.

"I know what I have to do, Adrianna. It *will* happen, but we shouldn't rush things. The Feldman family will soon find out that actions have consequences."

He got out of bed and went over to her, grabbing her by both arms.

"We have until Monday, Adrianna. Trust me, this will all be over soon and we can then return to Rome and get on with our lives. I have already made contact with someone here in London who can supply me with what I need. I'll set things in motion today. All you need to do is play your part well so that your new *lover* suspects nothing."

Adrianna grimaced at the word *lover*, groaned and stormed back to her room, leaving him to flop back on his bed, throw the duvet over his head and go back to sleep.

* * * * * *

The weekend had dragged, just as Simon had predicted. But now it was Monday morning and he was impatient to speak to Adrianna again. He had decided that, if today went well, he was going to ask her to spend the weekend with him at his parents' house. He felt sure they would approve of her, especially as she was Italian. He was certain his grandfather would have been happy with his choice. He also knew he was probably acting rashly, but did not care. Adrianna had completely captivated him and he was not going to let her slip through his fingers.

After dealing with the day's business commitments and checking that Chris had everything in hand with her new clients, he picked up the phone to call Adrianna, his heart pounding with excitement. She answered almost immediately and once again his heart leapt at the sound of her voice.

"I thought we could have dinner this evening," he said hopefully. "There's a French restaurant not far from my place, which is a favourite of mine. I'm sure you'll love it. Where are you staying? I'll come and pick you up."

Adrianna dissuaded him from that idea. She could not allow him to come anywhere near the flat. It would spoil everything.

"I'll come to your place this evening," she suggested, hoping that he had not noticed the momentary panic in her voice. "I don't want to inconvenience my friends and besides, it is out of your way. I can be with you at about seven-thirty, if that's OK?"

It was more than OK with Simon. The thought of being alone with her in his flat again excited him.

"That's perfect," he said. "*A più tardi, cara. Ciao.*" He then leant back in his seat with his head cradled in his hands, feeling decidedly pleased with himself.

CHAPTER 26

It was a perfect late summer evening. Earlier in the day it had rained hard, but by late afternoon the sun had come out, drying out the pavements and evaporating all signs of the downpour. It was now pleasantly warm with a gentle breeze.

Simon had left the office early so that he could take his time getting ready for Adrianna to arrive. He had bought wine – her favourite red – and had collected a bouquet of flowers from the local florist on the way home. He wanted tonight to be perfect. After all, he did not invite girls home to meet his parents every day.

He opened the French windows in the lounge to let in some air, also making it easy for Adrianna to appreciate the view of the gardens in the early evening sunshine. His housekeeper had been in earlier that day so the flat was immaculate. He often wondered what he would do without her. She was a woman of about fifty whose children had grown up and fled the nest, and she had been looking after Simon ever since he had come to London. She was very fond of him and fussed over him like a mother hen.

At just after seven-thirty he heard a taxi pull up outside the flat and, looking down from the balcony, saw Adrianna get out. She paid the driver, turned and looked up at him and waved. Moments later she was at his front door, which he had already opened. He had waited so impatiently for this moment that his excitement got the better of him, and, sweeping her up into his arms, he twirled her around before letting her down inside the hallway. He took her face in his hands and gave her a long, lingering kiss. She pushed him away gently, pretending to gasp for air before laughing and walking into the lounge. She noticed the open windows immediately and hurried onto the balcony.

"The gardens look wonderful," she said, turning back to smile at Simon. He rushed to her side and took her in his arms again, only this time she kissed him, running her fingers through his hair and holding his head captive. She playfully pushed him away again, satisfied in herself that she had full control.

"I'm starving," she said, running her finger down his chest and gazing into his eyes. "Shall we sample the delights of your favourite restaurant now, *bello*?"

He laughed and then remembered the flowers.

"I have something for you first," he said, holding up his finger to indicate for her to wait, and then disappeared into the kitchen. He returned almost immediately, triumphantly holding flowers out to her.

"*Grazie, caro*," she cooed, cradling the large bouquet in her right arm and stroking his face with the palm of her left hand. "They are beautiful, but I think I will have to put them in some water here until later."

She tilted her head to one side and winked at him.

Simon disappeared to the kitchen to put the flowers in a vase, and Adrianna closed her eyes and groaned softly. Did he really think that was all it took to buy her favour... a bunch of stupid flowers? She was tired of this game of charades.

On returning from the kitchen, Simon offered her his arm and together they left the flat. Out in the street, they walked towards the main road where it would be easier to hail a taxi. Cabs were always plentiful in this area, so they did not have long to wait. Adrianna was grateful that it was just a short drive to the restaurant. Being so close to him was becoming an ordeal and she was worried that she would let her true feelings escape and spoil everything.

Having waited so long for this opportunity, she did not want to be the one to ruin it.

The restaurant was modern in design, with beige walls adorned by abstract paintings. The room was light and airy and Simon had booked a table in the corner so that they could have some privacy. He wanted her full attention tonight.

The waiter showed them to their table and after exchanging greetings with Simon – whom he seemed to know quite well – he presented them with menus and took their drinks order. The menu was impressive and Simon ran through it with obvious enthusiasm, recommending the lobster, but Adrianna ordered lamb. She discreetly looked at her watch and wondered how long she was going to have to endure Simon's company this time.

Throughout the meal, Simon asked Adrianna questions about herself and her family. Which part of Italy did she come from and what did she do in Rome? She lied expertly, telling him that she had been brought up in Rome and now worked for a travel agency. She hoped this would explain her turning up in London so quickly after their first meeting. As the evening progressed, she managed to turn the focus around to Simon and his family. She felt more comfortable then and relaxed a little.

Eventually, Simon decided that the time was right to put his invitation to her. He took a mouthful of wine, swallowed, and then, picking up her hand, gazed into her eyes.

"Adrianna, I'd like to ask you something," he began.

She felt a rush of panic run through her.

"Of course, *caro*," she replied, hesitantly. "You can ask me anything."

He smiled warmly at her, feeling encouraged.

"I know we haven't known each other very long, but being with you feels so right. I would really love it if you would come and spend the weekend with me at my parents' home in Esher. It would mean a lot to me and I know they will love you."

He waited patiently for her answer, hoping desperately that she would not refuse him.

Adrianna could not believe her luck. They had been trying to decide how she could get Simon to provide them with easy access to Daniel Feldman and here he was offering his father to her on a plate, without any persuasion.

Her face lit up with excitement, which Simon, of course, mistook for pleasure at the prospect of spending time with him.

"I would love to meet your parents," she cooed. "It is so kind of you to ask me. Are you sure they will not mind?"

Simon rolled his eyes.

"How could they mind spending time with such a beautiful woman," he exclaimed. "My father, particularly, would love to talk to you. He is half Italian and you will remind him of his roots."

He raised her hand, which he was still holding, to his lips and kissed it tenderly. Adrianna gave him her best smile, while at the same time formulating a plan in her head. She could not wait to get back to the flat in Battersea and share her news. This changed everything.

CHAPTER 27

After his disastrous date with Chris, Mark spent the following week trying to figure out his priorities. The realisation of his feelings for Chris had been an unexpected complication and he was struggling to focus on what he had originally come to London for.

It worried him that he had been the cause of Chris's dramatic, unhappy departure from the restaurant and he knew he needed to put things right between them before he could get back on track. But so far, she was refusing to return his calls.

Nothing was going the way he had planned and he did not like it. The weekend came and went and he still had not heard from her, so he decided to take matters into his own hands, which was why he was sitting in the coffee house across the road from the Feldman & Son office on Monday morning, waiting for her to appear.

Tim had promised to ring him as usual as soon as he saw Chris leave the building, but it was nearly one o'clock and there had been no call. He was about to give up when his mobile rang. While talking to Tim, he saw Chris come out of the building and head towards the sandwich bar.

"I can see her Tim. I'm on it. Thanks," he said, ending the call. He jumped up so quickly that he nearly sent the table flying, but caught it just in time.

He hurried up the road behind Chris, calculating how he could give the impression he was casually catching up with her. He did not want her to think that he was a stalker, on top of everything else she probably imagined him to be.

Chris heard his footsteps and turned to see who was following her. Her face clouded over and, turning away again, she looked straight ahead, ignoring him.

"Go away Mark," she shouted over her shoulder. "I'm not in the mood for any more of your guessing games. Just leave me alone."

Mark caught up with her and, grabbing hold of her arm, spun her round to face him.

"Please listen to me Chris," he begged, while she struggled to free herself from his grip. "I'm sorry if I upset you on Saturday. It wasn't intentional, believe me."

Chris glared at him and he released his grip. People were looking at them as they passed by. Mark, however, was oblivious to the scene he was creating.

Chris hesitated for a moment, somewhat disarmed by the apparent sincerity of his apology.

"It wasn't a police interrogation Mark," she replied. "I was just trying to get to know you. Why are you so defensive?"

Her voice had softened now and Mark was almost tempted to

confide in her, but thought better of it.

"Come and have lunch with me," he said, taking hold of her hand. "There's a coffee house just across the road from your office. Give me half an hour at least. Please."

He looked deep into her eyes and Chris felt herself wavering.

"OK Mark, but I warn you, if you can't give me a good explanation for your behaviour then I'm out of there," she said earnestly.

As Mark held the door open for Chris, the waitress smiled at him, acknowledging his return but saying nothing. She was an avid reader of Mills & Boon and had a vivid imagination. This had all the signs of being a classic romance, she thought to herself.

Mark ignored her knowing glances and ordered two cappuccinos, while Chris looked at the menu. He watched her in silence, trying to decide what he should tell her.

The waitress reappeared with the coffees and took their order. Chris had not said a word to him since they had come in, so Mark decided to break the silence.

"Chris, I'm not necessarily the bad guy here," he began. "There are things about my life that are best left unsaid. My childhood wasn't exactly happy. My mother did her best as a single parent – my father having long since departed the scene – but when she met and married my stepfather, he and I didn't really hit it off. He was a bully and I hated the way he treated my mother. There were constant rows over my behaviour, and my mother was torn between standing up for me and trying to please him. As a result I became difficult to handle.

"Eventually, I was packed off to a boarding school in Broadstairs and I was more than happy to go. I just wanted to get as far away from home as possible, believing that my mother was just as much to blame for not standing up to him. It wasn't until I had graduated from college that something happened which caused me to look at things differently."

He paused, carefully editing the next words in his mind before they came out of his mouth. The waitress chose this moment to bring the ciabattas they had ordered.

"My parents decided to throw a party," he continued, "and during the evening I got talking to one of my mother's oldest friends. She was drunk and said something about my mother that she probably shouldn't have done. Something that I had been unaware of."

He stopped again and stared out of the window. Chris reached out and took his hand while waiting for him to continue.

"Of course," he said, eventually returning his attention to her, "I wasn't bothered whether I ended up dropping her in it or not, I just felt angry that I had been kept in the dark. I confronted my mother, as her friend hadn't given me any specifics, and asked her lots of questions, none of which she would answer. She just maintained that she had no idea what I was talking about.

"To cut a long story short, I got angry and Don, my stepfather, got involved. He had no idea, of course, what my problem was. He automatically assumed it was simply down to me causing trouble as usual. We argued, I packed my bag and came up to London earlier than I had planned."

He gazed into Chris's eyes, calculating that what he was revealing would stop her asking any further questions.

"After that," he concluded, "I spent most of my free time trying to work out what she was hiding, but I wasn't sure how to go about it. Money was tight when I first found work so I didn't go out much and had far too much time on my hands to brood. It wasn't until I started to really earn some money, after a brief spell in the City, that I started to go out and enjoy myself again and I pushed the mystery to the back of my mind. The extra money, when it came, was a further distraction, although I'm starting to wonder if I've been told the truth about that. Maybe she stole it and just pretended it was an inheritance!"

He withdrew his hand, smiled meekly at Chris and took a bite out of his ciabatta.

Chris returned the smile.

"Why didn't you just tell me all of this last Saturday?" she asked, picking up her own lunch. "We're not teenagers Mark, we're supposed to be adults. You really should learn to treat me as such. I might even be able to help you."

He shook his head wistfully.

"It's complicated Chris," he replied, wiping stray crumbs from the corner of his mouth. "It's not just me who's involved so I have to tread carefully. Besides, I still don't know what really happened, other than it caused a lot of arguments in the family. I need to handle it in my own way and I can't involve anyone else until I know for sure what I'm dealing with. Please understand that, and I promise I will tell you more when I can. Just not yet."

Chris was not sure what to say. This was the most he had told her since they first met. She settled for: "What are you going to do Mark? Have you a plan?"

She finished eating and watched his reaction with interest. He sighed and leant back in his chair.

"I don't know Chris. I'm very close to getting my answers but I need to think carefully about my next move. There's one thing I am certain of though, I don't want to lose you over it. I realised on Saturday, after you left me so abruptly, that you are just as important in my life as finding out about the past. Please trust me on this and say that you'll be patient. I know it's a lot to ask but I really don't want to involve you any more than I have done. Please Chris."

He looked deep into her eyes again and Chris could not help feeling a little worried for him. He had obviously been deeply affected by whatever it was he had learnt, and he was now in danger of letting it consume him. She just wished he would let her help him, but she was also intelligent enough to realise that she had already pushed him far enough. She thought for a while and then she smiled and tried to lighten the mood.

"OK Mark. I'll trust you... for now!" she declared. "But if I find out that this is just a ruse to keep me quiet, I swear I'll kill you, and there'll be no mystery about that!"

He laughed and, leaning across the table, took her face in both his hands and kissed her. The waitress sighed and glanced at the book she was reading surreptitiously behind the counter.

"Definitely Mills & Boon," she thought!

* * * * * *

From the reception desk, Tim watched Mark and Chris go into the coffee house. He was beginning to tire of Mark's cat and mouse game. He quite liked Chris and hoped that she was not going to become one of Mark's casualties. He looked at the clock on the wall by the lifts. It was nearly two o'clock, so it would not be long before she came back and he could find out what was going on.

Although he had known Mark all his life, they had only become close over the last few years. Being the younger of the two, Tim had always felt dominated. It was difficult to say no to Mark.

Half an hour later, Chris came into the reception area. Smiling briefly at him, she went over to the lift and eventually disappeared behind the closing doors. Tim grabbed his mobile and rang Mark.

"Well, Casanova, did you make up, or did she blow you out?" he snapped. The short burst of laughter at the other end of the line told Tim it had gone well. "Did you fess up or did you bottle it?" he continued.

"I sort of told her the truth, but economically," replied Mark. "I don't want her involved. I didn't tell her about you either. One revelation at a time!"

Tim gave a sarcastic huff.

"You're quite happy to drag *me* into your plots and schemes, though," he exclaimed, indignantly. "Talking of which, have you decided what you're going to do, now that you've found Daniel Feldman's lair, or are you just going to pop backwards and forwards on occasional sightseeing trips?"

There was a brief pause before Mark answered.

"Yes, I have decided. I'm going to confront him."

CHAPTER 28

Everything in Chris's garden was suddenly decidedly rosy. She and Mark had made-up and she was definitely beginning to make her mark at work. Simon was pleased with the proposals she had put together for her two prospective clients, and a third company on her list had also finally expressed interest.

She was feeling extremely optimistic about life. In this frame of mind, she decided to phone her mother and break the news to her that she had at last got herself a boyfriend. Hopefully, this would get her temporarily off her back. Her mother received the news with such enthusiasm that anyone overhearing their conversation would have thought that her daughter had just won the lottery.

"Oh Christina, that's wonderful news," she squealed. "When are we going to meet him dear? I can't wait to tell Susan Harris. I've had to put up with her continual bragging about Megan's brilliant fiancé, so it will be nice to have something to retaliate with. What does Mark do?"

Chris sighed. This was so typical of her mother.

"Mother, it's not a competition," she exclaimed. "In any case, Mark and I have only just started seeing each other. It's still early days. I don't want to scare him off by subjecting him to a cross examination by my family. As soon as I feel the time is right I'll be sure to introduce you to him. Until then, please try not to start planning a wedding!"

Her mother sniffed in indignation.

"Honestly Christina," she snapped, "you really should do something about those sarcastic tendencies of yours if you want to keep a man. It's not an attractive quality."

Chris ignored the comment, but the conversation had brought it home to her that, although Mark had confided in her about his uneasy relationship with his family, there was still so much about him she did not know – what he was doing when he was not with her being one of them. Nagging doubts began to creep back into her mind, but she wanted to trust Mark – for the time being.

After saying goodbye to her mother and replacing the receiver, she decided to catch up with Tessa, as she had not spoken to her since she and Mark had argued. She ought to let Tessa know that things were back on track now, to stop her worrying about her. She rang the number and propped the handset under her chin while she rummaged in her bag for her diary. The phone rang a few times while she glanced at the empty pages in the diary for that week. Her social calendar was looking decidedly sorry for itself. Finally, she heard Tessa's voice chime down the line.

"Hi Tessa," Chris greeted her, trying not to sound too pleased with

162

herself. "How are you? How's things with you and Peter?"

Tessa was uncharacteristically silent for a while, making Chris wonder if she had been inadvertently cut off.

"Chris, I'm so glad you phoned," she cried. "I wasn't sure whether to phone you or not, seeing as you were so upset over Mark. It's been awful, Chris. Pete and I split up. I caught him chatting up Cindy, one of the secretaries. He was asking her out, the rat."

She paused for breath and Chris could hear her voice waver. It surprised her as Tessa was usually so laid back about the men she dated, tending to get easily bored with them before quickly moving on to her next conquest. This was the first time she seemed to have been affected by a break-up.

"I'm so sorry Tess, I didn't realise you were that serious about him," Chris replied apologetically. "What did he say when you confronted him?"

Tessa had composed herself now and gave full flood to her anger.

"You won't believe it," she said indignantly, "but he actually tried to deny it, saying that he was just joking with her. What kind of an idiot does he take me for? I was standing right there when he asked her. It's so typical of my luck. The first time I decide I really like a guy he goes and plays me at my own game. Well, he can go to hell!"

Chris stifled a laugh. Tessa could be so melodramatic at times, but she did not deserve that kind of treatment.

"I feel guilty now about my news," she said.

"Don't be," Tessa replied. "I could do with something to cheer me up. What's happened?"

"I've decided to give Mark another chance," Chris continued. "He explained about his family, although I still have the feeling that there's more. However, I've decided to go with the flow and keep an open mind. I'll find out eventually."

She laughed at her own self-delusion. Even in such a short time she had come to realise how good Mark was at withholding the whole truth, but she was sure that she could be more than a match for him. She just had to be patient.

"Are you sure he's worth it, Chris?" Tessa asked. "Do you really need all that aggravation? In my experience guys who are economical with the truth about themselves are usually hiding something. Are you sure he's not married?"

Chris sighed.

"I'm not sure about anything, Tess," she admitted, searching her mind. "What I do know is that when we're together it feels right, despite everything. I'd like to give it another go and see what happens. If I bale out now, I'll never find out why he feels the need to be so mysterious and that will drive me insane. Maybe he's a secret agent after all!"

She laughed, provoking the same response from Tessa. It was good to hear her friend sound more like her old self.

"Let's get together one evening this week and swap stories about the failings of men," Chris suggested. "Like you always say, there's nothing like a bottle of wine and some good old fashioned bitching to drive away the demons."

Tessa readily agreed and they made arrangements to meet at Toppers on Thursday evening, Tessa having prior engagements before then.

After completing her phone calls, Chris went into the kitchen and opened the freezer. She stared at the sorry assortment of frozen meals inside and popped one into the microwave. As it cooked, she stood by the window, looking down into the small courtyard of a garden that she shared with her fellow tenants in the block. An elderly woman lived in one of the ground floor flats and had taken it upon herself to plant up some flowerpots and expertly arrange them around the square paved area. Being recently widowed, the woman now found herself spending too much time alone and the garden, such as it was, gave her something to focus on. While she never spent any time in the courtyard, Chris found looking at it surprisingly relaxing.

The ping from the microwave brought her back to reality.

While she was eating, Chris decided to invite Mark over for a meal, or rather a takeaway. There was no point in subjecting the poor guy to one of her frozen meals, not after the places he had taken her to.

She finished her meal and quickly cleared away the remnants. Then she picked up the phone and dialled Mark's number. It rang for quite a while, but just as she was about to hang up he answered.

"Mark, it's Chris," she said. "I was wondering if you would like to come over to my place tomorrow night for a meal. It'll only be a takeaway, I'm afraid. I'm not really known for my culinary skills, but the local Chinese does a mean Chow Mein."

There was a pause while Mark processed what she had said.

"Why not," he laughed. "A takeaway sounds great. After all, I wouldn't want to be responsible for you running the risk of poisoning me at such an early stage in our relationship! What time do you want me to be there?"

Chris felt a flutter of nerves in her stomach. For some reason she had not prepared herself for him to say yes, and now he had she felt mild panic.

"How about seven-thirty, is that OK?" she said, trying to sound as if she invited people round every day.

"Perfect," he said. "I'll see you then." He was still laughing as he hung up.

"Great," said Chris to herself, as she replaced the receiver. "Now I'm a source of amusement."

* * * * * *

Mark put his mobile back into his pocket and went into the kitchen to get another beer. Opening the fridge door he noted that there were only two left. "Tim really should keep an eye on his stocks," he thought, while he prised off the lid and resumed his prone position on the sofa.

He had been mulling over what day he should choose to put his plan into action and had just decided on Friday when Chris rang. It had been a welcome distraction. Getting so close to his final goal he was starting to worry that he might have overlooked something, but an evening with Chris would help him to relax and concentrate on the finer details.

While allowing himself the luxury of imagining himself alone with Chris, he resolved to address the dire lack of beers in the fridge and rang Tim, who had gone out for the evening with friends.

"Timbo," he said, as soon as he heard Tim's voice. "We need more beers, mate. Can you grab some from the off licence on your way home?"

Tim groaned loudly. His house guest was fast becoming a pain.

"Why couldn't you have got some earlier, Mark?" he protested. "You're the one with time on his hands. What have you been doing all day anyway? How's your diabolical plan coming along?"

"Stop moaning and just get the beers," snapped Mark, "and by the way, I'm out tomorrow night. Chris has invited me over to her place, so you'll have the place to yourself. Don't say I'm not good to you."

At the mention of Chris's name Tim's tone changed, and Mark noticed the hint of anxiety in his voice.

"Be careful Mark," Tim replied. "Chris is not like your usual casual conquests. You don't know how things are going to turn out yet and I'd hate for her, or you for that matter, to get hurt. By next week everything might have changed and you might very well be disappearing again. Have you really thought this through?"

Mark hesitated for a moment. He had thought of nothing else. Now that he had let Chris into his life things had admittedly become more complicated, but going back was not an option.

"Don't worry, Tim," he said reassuringly. "I know what I'm doing. Everything is under control, mate."

CHAPTER 29

Chris was in a blind panic. This would be her first attempt at entertaining a man and her mind had gone blank.

After getting in from work on the Wednesday evening she had spent half an hour soaking in the bath and almost as long trying to decide what to wear. Eventually, she had plumped for a figure-hugging red dress that she had bought for one of Tessa's parties a few months ago. After its initial outing she had put it back into her wardrobe and promptly forgotten about it – its relegation to the annals of history down to its apparent inability to attract any decent male attention. Tonight was its second chance.

At seven o'clock, she realised that she had yet to order the food. Fortunately, she had become quite friendly with Mr Liu at her local Chinese, as a result of the prodigious amount of time she had spent either eating in his restaurant or ordering his excellent takeaways. Mr Liu knew exactly what her favourites were, and when she rang he was ready with suggestions.

"You leave it to me," he said reassuringly. "I send you round nice selection. You will rock boyfriend's socks."

He started laughing and Chris imagined his toothy grin at the other end of the line. She thanked God for Mr Liu.

Checking that the table looked presentable, she wandered over to the CD player to select some suitable music. Her musical taste had always been out of step with her contemporaries. Not knowing what Mark's taste in music was, she decided her Best of Sade album was probably the least embarrassing. Yet another mystery, she thought to herself.

As the soft, dulcet harmonies of Sade's *'Your Love is King'* started to fill the room, Chris's mobile began to vibrate on the coffee table. She picked it up and checked the display. It was a text from Tessa. She smiled to herself and opened it.

"Hi sweetie. Go get him Tiger. Ring me later. Tessa x"

Chuckling, Chris switched off the phone and put it in her bedroom. She did not want any interruptions tonight. That goes for the landline too, she thought. The answerphone can deal with any calls.

Just before seven-fifteen the doorbell rang and, thinking it was the food, she opened the door with her purse in her hand. Instead, she was confronted by Mark's grinning face. He was dressed casually in black corduroy trousers with a white T-shirt under an expensive-looking black leather jacket.

Seeing the purse he started laughing.

"It's OK," he chortled, "I don't charge for my company, although it's an intriguing idea."

Chris blushed and threw the purse onto the telephone table. "Typical," she thought. "He hasn't even got through the door and I've managed to make myself look stupid."

While she was composing herself, Mark held out the bottle of wine he was holding.

"Thought this might be more useful than a bunch of flowers," he said smiling. "Sorry I'm a bit early. The traffic was lighter than I expected."

Chris smiled nervously and took the bottle from him. There was a moment's awkward silence, which was broken by Mark.

"Can I come in, or are we eating on the landing?" he asked, grinning again.

Realising that he was still standing outside, she ushered him in, apologising profusely for her manners.

"I'm so sorry," she said as he stepped inside, kissing her cheek as he passed. "This is the first time I've ever asked anyone round for a meal, apart from Tessa that is. She doesn't count though. I wasn't trying to impress her."

He laughed as she closed the door, offered to take his jacket and indicated for him to go through to the lounge.

As he walked into the room, his ears registered the sound of Sade singing 'Smooth Operator' and he gave a half smile to himself, hoping that Chris had not realised the irony of her choice of music.

When Chris finally followed him in, he was over by the CD player, looking through her collection. A wave of embarrassment rose inside her, as if he was rifling through her underwear drawer. She was acutely aware that her taste in music was sadly lacking.

"Interesting collection you have," Mark said, turning towards her, raising an eyebrow and grinning. Chris gave him a tolerant look before joining him.

"What are you into then?" she asked. "Rock? Heavy Metal?"

He ignored the implied sarcasm and smiled at her.

"Actually, I'm quite partial to Van Morrison," he replied. *"Into the Mystic* is a particular favourite. Don't suppose you have any of his albums, do you?"

The doorbell rang and Chris sighed with relief that this particular conversation could now be averted. Opening the door, she saw a teenage boy standing in front of her, with i-pod earphones firmly embedded in his ears. He was carrying a large bag of assorted containers, which he was now holding out to her. She recognised him as Mr Liu's son. He pulled the earphones out of his ears with his free hand and grinned at her.

"Hi," he said, with a wide smile that showed a gap in the middle of his top teeth. "Dad says there are two soups in there, some Chow Mein, sweet and sour chicken, seasonal vegetables, noodles and rice, along with a couple of his special desserts. He's also thrown in some spring rolls and prawn crackers as an extra, you being such a good customer. It comes to £31.50 in total."

Chris retrieved her purse from the hall table and paid him.

"Tell your dad thanks," she said, taking the bag from him.

"No worries," he replied, cheekily winking at her. "Enjoy!"

Chris closed the door and took the food into the kitchen, where she started to look for some dishes to serve things in.

Mark appeared in the doorway while she was desperately searching through her cupboards.

"Why don't you just leave the food in the containers," he suggested, as she emerged from the last cupboard having managed only to find a solitary serving dish. "No need to stand on ceremony on my account. Anyway, less to wash up at the end of the meal."

He walked over to where the bag lay unopened and picked it up, turned and headed towards the lounge. Chris conceded defeat and grabbing two glasses followed behind him, making a mental note to herself to do something about her lack of crockery, preferably before inviting anyone else round for a meal.

Mark unpacked the containers, taking off the lids as he went, until they were all open and displayed in the centre of the table. Chris had already laid out two plates and cutlery, so all that remained was for the food, which smelt really good, to be enjoyed.

As they ate, Chris found herself relaxing for the first time since Mark had arrived, and she allowed her eyes to linger on his face, taking in his deep blue eyes and casually arranged dark hair. His presence certainly made her feel warm and tingly inside, but it was still mixed with an uneasy feeling, which she was determined to ignore for the evening. There was plenty of time to find out what was bothering her. Tonight she intended to enjoy the moment.

He returned her gaze, smiling a little self-consciously.

"You're right," he said, trying to divert her attention. "This really is a mean Chow Mein. My compliments to the chef."

He helped himself to some more, while Chris topped up his glass with wine.

"The wine's not bad either," she replied, raising her eyebrows in mock surprise. "Looks like we have a winning combination. There's dessert too. Mr Liu has done us proud."

Then the telephone rang, but Chris ignored it, helping herself to some prawn crackers.

"Aren't you going to get that?" Mark asked.

"Absolutely not," she replied, gazing directly into his eyes. "It's probably my mother and she can wait. The answerphone can listen to her. Tonight is about us and I'm not going to let anything spoil it."

Mark feigned shock and laughing, reached across the table and took her hand in his.

"You really are quite a devious woman, aren't you," he said.

She squeezed his hand and rested her chin on her free hand.

"Yes, I am," she said, giving him her best attempt at a wicked smile.

After they had finished eating, Mark helped Chris clear the table. Walking into the kitchen, he threw the empty containers into the bin by the door and watched as she put the dirty plates and cutlery into a bowl of water in the sink.

"They can soak," she announced. "I'll deal with them later. Come and choose some music, as you didn't seem to be over impressed with my choice."

He obediently followed her into the lounge, but instead of going over to the CD player he pulled her to him and kissed her full and deeply on the lips. Chris felt herself swoon, but then, running her hands through his hair, she kissed him back.

"Wow," she said, when they eventually broke away. "That was worth the wait. I think you've been holding out on me."

He grinned at her and led her to the sofa where he gently pulled her down beside him.

"Mr Liu's dessert was good," he whispered into her ear, "but I can think of a better one."

Before she could reply, he gathered her in his arms and kissed her again. Chris felt her heart beating faster and knew that she was hopelessly addicted to him. All the doubts momentarily melted away, and putting her hand on his face, she purred into his ear.

"You know, you don't have to go home tonight... if you don't want to."

He swept her hair to one side and lightly brushed her neck with his lips.

"I don't want to," he whispered.

CHAPTER 30

The tube was packed as usual, but Chris managed to find a seat and was now in her own little world, bathed in the warm afterglow.

Mark had still been asleep when she left for work. He had looked so peaceful that she decided not to wake him, but to leave a note on the pillow saying that she would call him later that morning.

The tube rattled to a halt, rudely jolting her out of her thoughts. Realising that it was her stop she got up, pushed her way through the mass of people, and headed towards the doors. She was not sure how she was going to keep her mind focussed today. However, she knew that once she got to the office she could slot into work mode and the memories of her romantic evening would be neatly filed away in her mind until she was free to retrieve them.

She swept through the office doors and threw a cheery good morning at Tim, before getting into the lift. Tim looked up from the newspaper he was surreptitiously reading below the desk, watched her disappear behind the doors and smiled. When Mark had failed to come home last night he had guessed the reason and Chris's demeanour confirmed his supposition.

Simon was also in a good mood. Adrianna had agreed to spend the weekend at his parents' house and, as he had thought, his father had been delighted by his choice of an Italian girl. Everything in his garden was also rosy. He called Chris into his office, once his morning ritual of post reading, email checking and coffee was complete, and they began to run through the work schedule for the day. Chris noticed his new relaxed mood and, after contemplating whether or not to comment on it, decided that she was not going to last the day without knowing the cause.

"You're unusually cheerful for this time of the morning," she ventured. "Have you had some good news?"

There was a brief pause before he answered and Chris momentarily wondered if she had spoken out of turn, but a broad smile broke across his face and he leant back in his chair, cradling the back of his head between his entwined hands.

"Well, since you've asked, I think I've finally found the girl of my dreams," he said. "We met that evening in Rome, after you and I got back to the hotel. She was in the bar and we hit it off straight away. Her name's Adrianna and she's Italian. Seems like I'm carrying on the family tradition with its links to Italy. I'm introducing her to my parents this weekend."

Chris cast her mind back to that night and her suspicious female mind automatically wondered why a woman would be on her own in a bar at that time of night, let alone striking up a conversation with a stranger. Maybe Italian women were less reserved.

She brushed the thought aside almost at once. It was not her place to judge, especially as she still had so many unanswered questions concerning Mark. She should be happy for Simon, as he obviously liked this Adrianna and, after all, she was not aware of all the facts. She returned his smile and said that she hoped that things would work out well.

Once back in her own office, Chris started thinking again about that evening in Rome. He had definitely been more than a bit tipsy that night, as had she. Meeting someone in a bar in his inebriated state would surely have impeded his judgement, and the following morning he had made no mention of meeting any dream woman. Now she had miraculously turned up in London and he was introducing her to his parents. She realised she was probably letting her imagination run away with her. Why was she suddenly so suspicious of everyone? First it had been Mark, and now this mysterious Italian woman. It was starting to become a habit.

Dismissing Simon's personal life from her mind, she began to concentrate on her workload for the day. For the rest of the morning her phone refused to stop ringing and by lunchtime her ears felt as if they were burning from constant contact with the receiver. She was just about to put on her jacket and head off towards the sandwich bar when her mobile rang. Glancing at the display, she took a sharp intake of breath when she saw Mark's name staring up at her. She had forgotten to phone him.

"Hello Sleeping Beauty," she said, attempting not to sound flustered. "You're awake then."

Mark laughed at her playful sarcasm.

"I should hope so," he replied. "Otherwise I'm in danger of missing the whole day. I found your note. When you didn't ring I thought you were avoiding me, so I decided I'd better ring you in case you were trying to do a runner!"

"Of course not," Chris said, laughing back. "I've just been incredibly busy this morning. Life doesn't revolve around you, you know." She softened her tone. "Anyway, how are you today? No regrets I hope. I had a great evening."

"Are you kidding?" came the reply. "Best meal I've had for ages and the dessert was... amazing! I've been thinking about you all morning. What are you doing later?"

Chris remembered her date with Tessa.

"Oh Mark," she apologised. "I'm so sorry, but I promised Tessa I'd spend the evening with her. She's broken up with Pete and needs cheering up. We can meet up on Friday though, if you like. Or maybe at the weekend?"

There was a brief moment of silence on the line before Mark answered her, his previously light-hearted tone now sounding slightly annoyed.

"Sorry, I've got something planned for Friday that can't wait," he said sharply. "As for the weekend, I'll have to get back to you on that. I'm not sure if I'll be around. Have a nice evening though and I'll catch up with you later." Then, realising he was letting his selfishness get the better of him, he added: "Oh and Chris... I really did have a great time last night."

Chris felt a wave of disappointment pass through her and she was about to question Mark as to what he thought was more important than seeing her when he hung up. She could not say exactly what it was, but her instincts still told her that something was not quite right. The old familiar doubts had returned as she put her phone in her bag, grabbed her jacket and headed off to get some lunch.

CHAPTER 31

Chris had planned to meet Tessa at her flat that evening, but at the last minute, owing to an unexpected problem with some promotional material, she needed to work late and asked Tessa if she minded meeting her at Toppers instead. It was, therefore, about seven o'clock when she finally walked through the door.

"Chrissie, over here," Tessa cried, standing up and waving her arm wildly, while raising her voice over the noisy chatter. Chris saw her and, waving back, made her way towards her table. The place was busy for a Thursday night and the only table Tessa had managed to find was in a corner not easily seen from the door. When Chris finally reached her friend, Tessa threw her arms around her and sat back down in her seat. She had bought a bottle of wine, which was already almost empty. Chris took her coat off and sat down next to her, raising her eyebrows as she noticed the bottle.

"How long have you been here?" she asked, smiling. "Looks as if I've got some catching up to do."

Tessa laughed and poured the remaining wine into a glass for Chris.

"About half an hour, sweetie" she replied, holding the empty bottle up and examining its lack of content. She smiled broadly at Chris. "I desperately need to obliterate that rat from my mind, so let's order another one."

Chris took a quick sip from her glass and made her way to the bar. It was extremely crowded, so she had to wriggle her way to the front in order to catch the barman's eye. Finally he saw her and, as he approached her, she asked for a bottle of Chardonnay. When he returned with the bottle Chris noted the way his eyes were scanning her and found herself feeling slightly uncomfortable, especially when he winked at her.

Casting her mind back to the last time she was in here with Tessa she recalled how easily her friend had dealt with the barman's flirtations and decided that she really should learn to relax more.

After hastily paying, Chris manoeuvred her way back to Tessa and placed the bottle on the table before reclaiming her seat. Tessa picked up the bottle, topped up Chris's glass and poured herself one. She proceeded to gulp it down.

"Steady, Tess," Chris exclaimed. "You'll be pie-eyed by the time we leave at this rate! Slow down and tell me all about Pete. Is he going out with that Cindy now?"

Tessa sighed and looked down at her glass, rolling it backwards and forwards between her fingers. The smile disappeared from her face.

"I know you think that I don't take relationships that seriously, always playing the field, but this time I really did like him Chris," she said sadly, lifting her brown eyes up at Chris and wiping away a solitary tear. "I suppose this is my come uppance for treating past boyfriends so badly. How could I have been so stupid?"

Chris felt intensely sorry for Tessa. She was usually so bubbly and self-confident and this was unlike her. She was at a loss for words, so put her arm around her friend instead.

Tessa suddenly sat bolt upright and, forcing a smile back onto her face, tapped the table in front of her hard with both her hands.

"Well," she declared, "that's the last time I'm going to let that happen. Men are a pain and not worth worrying about. Drink up, sweetie, and tell me about your date with Mark. There's no reason why we should both be miserable."

Chris removed her arm and gave her a warm smile.

"OK," she said, leaning back in her chair, "We had a great evening. He was funny and charming, and…. he stayed the night."

She waited for Tessa to digest what she had said. Tessa's mouth was open.

"Finally!" she eventually squealed. "I was beginning to think you weren't normal." A wicked gleam then appeared in her eyes. "Was it worth the wait, sweetie?" she continued. "When are you seeing him again?"

Chris sat forward, put her elbows on the table and rested her chin in her hands.

"That's the problem," she replied. "When I said I couldn't see him tonight and offered to meet up with him tomorrow or at the weekend, he went all mysterious on me again, saying he had 'something urgent to do' that couldn't wait." She imitated Mark's tone and made invisible quote marks in the air to emphasis the statement.

"He was even reluctant to commit to the weekend," she continued. "Honestly, Tess. I like him a lot, but I really don't know where I stand with him. It's starting to mess with my head and my imagination has gone into overdrive. If that wasn't bad enough, Simon told me today that he met the love of his life in the hotel bar when we were in Rome a couple of weeks ago and is taking her home to meet his parents this weekend. How crazy is that? One guy tells me too much and the other not enough."

She threw her hands up in the air in frustration, before letting them fall back into her lap.

"I think you're right, Tess," she concluded. "Men *are* a pain!"

* * * * * *

Mark felt put out after his phone call with Chris. After their night together he had expected her to be falling over herself to see him again and not to blow him out for a girlfriend. It was another disagreeable new experience for him. He had wanted to see her before his confrontation with Daniel Feldman on Friday, in case it proved to be his last chance. Now he was not sure when, or indeed if, he would see her again. In that frame of mind, he dialled Tim's number.

"Timbo," he snapped, when the phone was answered, "Whatever your plans are for later, cancel them. I need to have my mind focussed for tomorrow night, so meet me in the usual place at about six so I can run things through with you. It'll be better than talking to myself. Drinks are on me."

With that he hung up, leaving Tim uttering oaths at his desk.

* * * * * *

After about an hour Chris had almost caught up with Tessa on the wine front and the two were now giggling helplessly as they swapped unflattering opinions of the men in their lives. Tessa was back to her usual self and beginning to expel Pete to the darker recesses of her mind. The flirty attentions of the barman had also served to distract her while she was ordering another bottle of Chardonnay.

"I'm sorry I was so melodramatic earlier," she apologised, now wiping tears of laughter from her eyes and cheeks. "I promise it won't happen again... tonight anyway!" She started laughing once more, causing Chris to erupt as well.

"I'm glad to hear it," Chris replied, trying to control her giggles. The wine was certainly taking effect now but she did not care. It was good to spend time with someone who was open with her and not making her feel as if every question was a crime. She raised her glass to Tessa.

"To the sisterhood, and to hell with worrying about men!"

"I'll drink to that," replied Tessa, picking up her own glass.

The two women laughed again and both swallowed a large mouthful of wine.

As Chris's gaze casually scanned the room, her relaxed mood changed with a start. She shook her head in disbelief as first she caught sight of Mark, who was making his way through the crowd of people near the bar towards the exit door, then she spotted his drinking companion.

The wine bar had been so crowded that, from their shielded position in the corner and due to the throng of people around the bar, she had not noticed them earlier. It took a moment to realise, through the effect of the alcohol, that Mark's friend was none other than Tim Myers.

Hurriedly shifting her mind into gear, she called out to Mark and waved, but the hubbub in the bar drowned out her voice and before she knew it the two of them had disappeared through the door and out into the night.

"That was Mark," she exclaimed, turning back to Tessa with wide eyes. "He was with Tim Meyers from reception. I didn't even know they knew each other. What the hell is going on Tess? I feel as if I'm part of some kind of game where everyone knows the rules except me."

Tessa looked towards the door but even if she had been able to focus properly, the two men were long gone. She returned her gaze back to Chris, who had rummaged through her bag for her mobile and, finding it, had dialled Mark's number. It went straight into voice mail.

"Damn," hissed Chris, ending the call and throwing her phone back into her bag. "His phone's switched off and I don't have Tim's number."

Her head started to throb and she realised that she had drunk more than enough for one night. She was having trouble thinking clearly.

"I think I need to go home, Tess," she said, reaching for her coat. "I need a clear head to think about this. There's something not quite right going on and I've got to get to the bottom of it."

Tessa nodded and stood up, swaying violently as the sudden change in altitude hit her.

"Whoa," she exclaimed, holding on to the table. "Do you think I could stay at your place tonight, sweetie? It's nearer than mine and I'm really not sure if I'm going to make it home on my own." She fumbled for her coat and bag and then leant heavily on Chris's arm. "I'm sure whatever Mark's explanation is it can keep until tomorrow," she slurred.

Chris looked at her friend with concern. She felt decidedly tipsy herself but Tessa was in a worse state.

"Of course you can," she replied. "I'm certainly not letting you make your own way home in that condition. I told you that you'd end up pie-eyed drinking that fast."

Tessa let go of Chris's arm and gave her a drunken grin, holding up one hand in acknowledgement, while trying to put her coat on with the other. She was having trouble finding the arms so Chris helped her.

The two of them left the bar with Tessa holding on to Chris to stop herself from stumbling. One or two people broke off from their conversations to smile in their direction, but Tessa was oblivious to the attention she was drawing to herself.

Once outside, the fresh air cleared Chris's head a little. Unfortunately, it had the opposite effect on Tessa, who declared that she was feeling decidedly queasy. Fearing that her friend might either be sick or pass out, Chris looked around for a taxi and was relieved to see one heading in their direction. Hailing it, she propped Tessa up to try to disguise her inebriated state, fearful that the driver might be reluctant to take them. Luckily he accepted the fare, and they were soon on their way back to Chris's flat, Tessa with her head on her friend's shoulder and Chris thinking about how she was going to confront Tim the next day.

CHAPTER 32

Chris slowly let the light filter through her eyelids as the sound of her alarm clock drifted into her consciousness.

Reaching over, she turned it off, then sank back onto her pillow and tried to focus. Rubbing her eyes with one hand, the events of last night gradually started to re-form in her mind and she gave a low moan. Although the sun was firmly hidden behind a bank of cloud, the light was still strong enough in her present condition to make her want to close her eyes again.

Remembering that Tessa had stayed over, she glanced towards the other side of the bed. On getting home it was obvious that Tessa's consciousness was not going to hold up much longer, so Chris had simply laid her on the bed, undressed her down to her underwear and tucked her in. She was now lying on her stomach with one arm dangling over the side of the bed, breathing heavily in a deep sleep.

Chris gently shook her a couple of times and then waited while her friend came round. Tessa grunted, rolled over, rubbed her eyes and then looked at Chris with a dazed expression on her face.

"God, what happened last night, sweetie?" she mumbled. "My head feels as if it's been run over by a steamroller."

As reality began to take hold, she dragged herself up onto her elbows and looked at the clock.

"Oh no!" she cried on seeing the time. "I'm going to be late. I need to get back to my flat and change for work."

Chris watched as Tessa jumped out of bed, promptly sitting down again and holding her head with one hand while steadying herself with the other.

"I'm so sorry about last night, Chris," she said quietly, trying not to aggravate her throbbing head. "I haven't been that drunk since I first left home and decided to celebrate my freedom. I really should know better, especially over a man!"

Chris laughed and, getting out of bed, walked over to Tessa's side and gently helped her to stand up.

"Would you like me to run you a bath or shower?" she asked. "You can borrow some of my clothes if you like. They might be a bit long on you, but it will save you some time."

Tessa let the idea seep in and decided that Chris was probably right. Declining Chris's offer of help, she gingerly made her way towards the bathroom and turned on the shower, letting it run while she carefully removed the underwear she had been sleeping in.

While Tessa was in the shower, Chris sorted out clean clothes for her and put the kettle on for coffee. She felt quite sober now, despite drinking well over her normal self-imposed limit. She put it down to the shock of seeing Mark in the wine bar last night, and now a bewildering array of emotions was welling up inside her. While the kettle boiled she started to mull over her options. She dialled Mark's number again, but his mobile once more went straight to voice mail. She cursed and hung up.

* * * * * * *

Mark had spent the evening discussing his plans with Tim. He was not sure why, as he did not need his approval, but it helped to get things straight in his mind by saying them out loud to someone, and Tim was the only one he trusted.

He had switched his mobile off to avoid distraction, mainly because he did not want to have to lie to Chris again, if she happened to call. He was not expecting her to, as she had told him that she was going to be at Tessa's place all night. To his mind, she had made it quite clear that her friend was her main concern at the moment, but he did not want to chance it. Women! He would never truly understand them.

However, Tim had been less than encouraging, suggesting that Mark should forget his insane machinations. Over the last few weeks he had seen how Mark had started to become obsessed, he said, and he was beginning to worry about the effect it was having. He could not see it ending well.

Mark had not responded favourably to his opinion.

* * * * * * *

On Friday morning, Tim was seated behind the reception desk as usual, drinking his first coffee of the day. He had decided that if Mark was going to ignore his advice then he was on his own with his mad intentions. He was definitely not going to let himself be dragged into something that he did not feel comfortable with.

He found himself looking at the clock and realised it was not going to be that easy. Knowing that Mark was going to instigate his plans that evening, he also knew it was going to be impossible for him to concentrate on anything else until it was all over, one way or the other.

He was preoccupied when Chris walked through the main doors, only registering her presence at the last moment. She hurried past him giving him a cursory glance but said nothing. The expression on her face was accusatory.

She disappeared behind the lift doors, leaving Tim to wonder what he had done.

* * * * * *

The Italian was sitting on Adrianna's bed, cleaning and checking one of two revolvers, while at the same time watching her pack for her weekend with Simon's parents.

"I don't know why you're bothering to pack so much," he said lazily. "You won't be staying long, unless you've done something stupid… like actually started to care for the idiot!"

He put down the gun and glared at her. Adrianna stopped packing and swung round to glare back at him.

"I feel nothing for him but disgust and the sooner the job is done the better!" she hissed. "I don't want to be in his company a minute longer than I have to, but if I don't have enough luggage with me he'll become suspicious. Use your head and concentrate on what *you* have to do, instead of criticising me."

"I'm sorry," he huffed, turning his attention back to the gun. "It's just I don't want you to get distracted. Now that it's nearly over, I don't want anything to go wrong."

He heard her angrily zip up her case.

"I'm not a weak-minded English girl who swoons at the slightest smile from a good-looking man," Adrianna hissed at him. "If it all goes wrong tonight it won't be because of me. Just make sure you are up to the job and everything will be fine. I should be at the house by about seven, according to Simon, so make sure you are in place by then. I don't intend to play happy families all night."

Turning back to her case, she grabbed it and jerked it onto the floor. Realising that it was not wise to antagonise her, he tried another tack.

"Adrianna, this would have been over long ago if mamma hadn't fallen seriously ill and felt the need to forgive him," he said, trying not to show his frustration. "I can't be as forgiving as her. I respected her wishes at the time, but when she died it meant that I could finally complete what I started six years ago. I need you to help me. We both owe it to papa to make sure that Feldman pays for his treachery, no matter what the personal cost."

Adrianna stood motionless, staring at the wall, before turning to face her brother.

"I'm meeting Simon at his office at five," she said, her voice more composed. "Did you manage to get a car?"

"Of course I did," he snarled indignantly. Adrianna ignored his angry tone.

"You can drive me to the office," she said. "Simon doesn't know you, so you should be able to follow us without him noticing anything. He parks his car across the road from the building in the permit holders bay, so we'll be easy to spot when we come out. Just make sure you are not too obvious while you are waiting for us." She glanced at her watch. "We still have some time to kill, so how about some lunch? I'm not doing this on an empty stomach!"

He agreed begrudgingly and handed her the second gun, which she put in her handbag. If nothing else, his sister was extremely practical.

CHAPTER 33

Chris was finding it hard to focus, and as the day wore on her concentration gradually gave up on her altogether. All she could think about was seeing Mark with Tim, and why neither of them had mentioned the fact that they knew each other – and pretty well, judging by what she had seen. She had even joked with Mark about the cheeky way in which Tim bantered with her each morning, but never once had he said anything about their acquaintance.

She had thought that they were past all the secrecy – obviously she had been mistaken.

As soon as the clock in her office registered five o'clock, she grabbed her coat and bag and after putting her head around Simon's door to wish him a good weekend, marched down the corridor towards the lift, deep in thought about what she was going to say to Tim. Because of this, as the lift doors opened she failed to notice the strikingly beautiful, dark haired woman emerge and the two women almost collided.

"I'm so sorry," apologised Chris. "I was miles away. Can I help you?"

The woman looked her up and down, trying to determine her importance, and then gave her a faux smile – the kind of smile that women reserve for each other when they are feigning politeness.

"Possibly," the woman finally replied. "I'm here to meet Simon. Could you show me where his office is? He's expecting me. I'm Adrianna."

She held out a well-manicured hand towards Chris, who shook it briefly, immediately deciding there was something about this woman she definitely did not like. Surely this was not the woman Simon was taking to meet his parents she thought, as she led Adrianna towards Simon's office, although it was none of her business if he had decided to let his eyes rule his head. Reaching his office, she opened the door and showed the woman in.

"Adrianna," Simon exclaimed, jumping up and beaming from ear to ear. He gave her a warm kiss on both cheeks. "Come and sit down, I've just got one or two things to finish and then we can be on our way. I see you've met my assistant, Christina Newman."

He smiled at Chris, obviously seeking her approval. Chris hoped that later he would not ask her outright to give him an opinion of his choice – she had always been a rubbish liar.

She smiled back, said it was good to have met Adrianna and then took her leave. She had important business of her own to attend to which could not wait.

* * * * *

Tim had also been clock-watching. If he could get away promptly he might stand a chance of catching Mark before he made a fool of himself and did something he was going to regret.

At five o'clock, he had begun to get ready to leave, but as he got up from his seat a beautiful Italian woman walked through the entrance door, pulling a wheeled suitcase behind her, and so he dutifully sat down again and switched on his welcome smile. She had not smiled back.

"I'm here to see Simon Feldman," she said, with a toss of her dark hair. "He's expecting me, so please inform him that Adrianna is here." Without waiting for a reply, she had parked herself on one of the visitors' chairs, elegantly crossing her legs and gazing out of the window as she did so.

Tim watched her glide across to the seat, his mouth wide open, picked up the phone and dialled Simon's internal number. The reply was immediate and the instruction to show her up given with enthusiasm.

"Mr Feldman says to please go up," Tim informed Adrianna, unable to take his eyes off her as she got up and walked towards him. "Just take the lift and press the first floor button. Someone will show you the way from there."

"Thank you. I will leave my case here," Adrianna replied, positioning her suitcase by the side of the reception desk and making her way over to the lift.

Tim had just been about to mention that it was probably better if he put the case behind the desk, when the lift door opened and Adrianna stepped in. With her image still lingering in his mind, he tried to imagine what could be so urgent for Feldman to see a client so late on a Friday evening. He was usually the first one out of the door at the start of the weekend. He decided that, whatever the reason, she was worth waiting for… even if she was a tad pushy.

He wheeled her case to a less prominent place behind the desk and put on his jacket.

Just as he opened the main door to leave, Chris came rushing out of the lift. Before he had time to realise who it was approaching him, she grabbed him by the arm and forced him up against the wall of the reception.

"Stay right where you are, Tim Meyers," she hissed. "You have some explaining to do, and don't try and fob me off with any stories either. I saw you two together last night in Toppers. What's going on?"

Tim, still stunned by her sudden attack, managed to release himself from her grip and straightened the arm of his jacket. "The woman is obviously mad," he thought.

"What on earth do you mean?" he replied, playing dumb. "I really don't know what you're talking about. You'll have to be more specific I'm afraid."

"You know exactly what I'm talking about," Chris spat back, unperturbed by his feigned ignorance. "You and Mark. He must know that you work here and you know me, but neither of you said anything to me about knowing each other. I can just about accept *you* not mentioning it, but *he* has no excuse. You are going to tell me right now the reason for all this secrecy or I might be tempted to tell Simon that maybe he should think twice about the person running his reception desk."

Tim had had enough of covering up and lying for Mark. This was getting out of hand, particularly now that he could find himself being the loser.

"OK," he finally said. "It wasn't my idea to keep it all from you. He can be really persuasive when he puts his mind to it. He's always been able to manipulate me, perhaps it's time to stand up to him."

As Tim proceeded to tell Chris exactly what Mark was up to, with a brief history of why, including his part in the whole affair, she listened with growing disbelief.

"Oh my God," she exclaimed, glaring at Tim. "And you're letting him go through with it? How could you be so irresponsible, Tim? The timing is completely wrong. Simon is taking his new girlfriend to meet his parents this weekend, so they're all going to be there. He'll be walking into a lion's den and he won't be prepared for it. The Feldmans are practically an empire and this will just cause them to close ranks in order to protect their interests... and each other. You idiot!"

Tim felt a sudden surge of anger. It was not his fault if Mark was stupid enough to think he could take on the might of the Feldmans. He had tried to warn him.

"What do you expect me to do about it?" he snapped. "You know how stubborn and single-minded he is. He was never going to listen to me, or anyone."

Chris reflected for a moment and a disturbing thought entered her mind.

"Was I part of his plan to get to the Feldmans?" she asked slowly, not really needing the answer confirmed.

Tim hesitated. It really should not have to be him having this conversation with Chris and he was unsure what to tell her. But she had a right to know.

"Yes. It certainly started out that way, but if it's any consolation it didn't go according to plan," he said. "He didn't expect to like you so much and now I think he's actually beginning to fall in love with you, only he'd kill me for saying that."

Chris was staring at him in shock and tears were forming in the corners of her eyes. He instantly regretted what he had said and found himself wanting to comfort her.

"I think he's been on the verge of telling you the truth, especially after you walked out on him that time," he continued in a softer tone, "but the longer it went on, the harder it became. He didn't want to lose you again and he honestly didn't want to get you mixed up in his plans, in case something went wrong and you ended up being implicated. You have to believe that Chris. Be angry with him by all means, but he really does care about you."

Chris wiped the tears from her eyes and, after digesting everything Tim had said, straightened up to her full height and looked him directly in the eyes.

"Right," she said. "Here's what we are going to do. I'll deal with my relationship with Mr Dempster later, but I'm damned if I'm going to let him make the biggest mistake of his life without at least trying to stop him."

The lift doors opened and Simon appeared with Adrianna on his arm. Chris cursed silently to herself and turned to face them, smiling.

"Still here?" Simon asked, raising his eyebrows. "I thought you'd be long gone by now. Tim too I see. I'm even more surprised to see you still here." Then turning to Adrianna he asked: "Did you say you left your case here?"

Adrianna nodded towards Tim.

"I asked your receptionist to look after it," she replied, smiling at Simon.

Tim rushed forward, glad to break the tension between himself and Chris, and retrieved the suitcase from behind the desk. Simon took it from him and putting his free arm around Adrianna's waist, wished Chris and Tim a good weekend and guided Adrianna out through the door into the street, pulling her suitcase behind him.

"They're going to have a head start," Chris moaned. "Do you have a car? If so where is it?"

"Yes I do, but it's at my flat," Tim replied. "I don't use it for work because of the congestion charge and the parking. We don't all have generous benefactors!"

"Then we'll have to grab a taxi and get back to your flat as soon as possible," Chris calculated. "We're going to get caught up in the Friday night rush to get out of London, but then so are they. Let's hope they are not in as much of a hurry as we are."

She grabbed hold of Tim's arm and propelled him through the door. The adrenalin was beginning to pump through her veins. It was going to be a close call.

CHAPTER 34

Having decided that Friday evening would be a good time to execute his plan, Mark turned his attentions to the question of how he was actually going to carry it out.

He figured that, by waiting until Friday, he would stand a better chance of finding Feldman and his wife at home, when they should be settling down for a nice cosy weekend. He hoped to take them by surprise and gain the upper hand. This thought pleased him immensely.

Once he had formulated and rehearsed an exact scenario in his mind, the rest of the day seemed to pass in slow motion. This gave him time to reflect on recent events.

Over the last few weeks his life seemed to have changed completely. Whereas, in the past, he had only ever thought about himself, he now found himself thinking about someone else… Chris. In fact, he could not stop thinking about her and it was proving to be a big distraction. He needed a clear head today.

As the afternoon slowly gave way to early evening, Mark went into his room and changed out of his jeans and T-shirt. The occasion, he thought, demanded smart clothes to add to his sense of drama. He checked himself in the mirror and, satisfied with his appearance, left the flat and made his way down to his car, running in his mind his carefully crafted script.

The rush hour was in full swing and his drive to Esher was painfully slow. Once or twice he felt a surge of doubt, but managed to push it out of his mind and focus on the task ahead. After tonight everything would change, but whether for better or worse he could not say.

Eventually, he pulled up across the road from Daniel Feldman's house. Switching off the engine, he looked at his watch. It was just after seven. His heart began to beat much faster and he had to take a few deep breaths to regain control of himself. Taking a final lungful of air, he began to open the car door, but as he did so, another car appeared behind him and turned into the Feldmans' driveway.

Mark closed his door quickly, hoping he had not been spotted. Not recognising the car, he sunk down in his seat and discreetly watched its occupants climb out.

"Damn!" he cursed out loud on seeing Simon. "What the hell is he doing here?"

* * * * * *

Adrianna's brother had followed Simon's car all the way to Esher, keeping a safe distance. He parked his car just around the corner from the house and was deciding on the best way to enter the grounds unseen.

Adrianna had played her part well and he knew it was now up to him. Although it was late summer it would not be dark until at least eight o'clock, so it could still be possible for someone to spot him if he was not careful.

Adrianna had learnt from Simon that Feldman had an office on the ground floor of the house, with a French window overlooking the rear lawn. They agreed this was a sensible place for him to break in, believing that, as soon as Adrianna and Simon arrived, the family would probably adjourn to the lounge, leaving the office empty. Once the pleasantries were over, she would find a way of getting Daniel into his office. But he had to go in there alone.

Surrounding the front garden of the house was a fairly high hedge. It enclosed several large shrubs, scattered randomly across the extensive front lawn. They offered ample protection from prying eyes. Waiting until the coast was clear, he slipped into the garden and hid behind a group of the larger shrubs.

He had not, however, totally escaped notice.

Simon's arrival had thrown Mark into a state of near panic and he needed to calm down and reassess his options. As he desperately tried to collect his thoughts, he also became aware of something, or someone, moving across the garden. Although the hedge made it impossible for him to identify the cause, the movement was certainly enough to add fuel to his anxiety and he wanted to know what it was. If it turned out to be a member of the family he would have to wait until they were inside the house. He needed everyone to be in one place. He did not want any surprises.

Getting out of his car, he quietly closed and locked the door, trying not to attract attention. Looking around him, he casually strode towards the front garden. The front door was closed and it was easy for him to dart behind the shrubs and make his way around to the back of the house unnoticed. He was just in time to see a dark-haired man peer through a set of French doors, expertly force one of them open and disappear inside.

CHAPTER 35

Simon had enjoyed every minute of the long drive down to Esher. Unperturbed by the amount of traffic on the roads, he had simply loved spending more time with Adrianna.

Inhaling her perfume, he had congratulated himself on his good fortune, sliding his hand onto her knee and smiling at her.

Adrianna, however, had not been inclined to return the sentiment, and tactfully removed his hand, pointing out that he should be watching the road. She wanted the whole affair to be over, so that she could resume her life back in Rome. The traffic only added to her agony.

When they finally turned into the driveway of the house, she let out a silent sigh of relief and prepared herself to become the perfect girlfriend and guest.

Turning to Simon, she smiled warmly and expressed delight at the appearance of his parents' home. He beamed back at her and, getting out of the car, went around to her side, opened her door and offered her his hand. She gracefully got out of the car, no mean achievement given how low the Porsche seats were and the shortness of her skirt.

He retrieved their cases from the boot and they made their way towards the house.

"That's odd," said Simon, as they reached the front door. "Mother always hears the car when I arrive and usually has the door open to greet me. She's always so pleased when I come down for the weekend, complaining that I don't visit them nearly enough. She's probably right."

He got out his key and opened the door, calling out as he did so. Adrianna followed him in and as Simon closed the door behind them, Daniel Feldman appeared in the hallway, stifling a yawn.

"Hello, I didn't realise it was so late. I'm afraid you caught me taking a late-afternoon nap," he apologised, holding out his hand to Adrianna. "You must be Adrianna, my dear. It's nice to meet you. Simon has told us so much about you that I feel I already know you. Come into the lounge and make yourself comfortable. You must be tired after the drive down. It's been a while since I've had to brave the traffic from London but I can still remember what a nightmare the Friday night exodus used to be."

He led the way into the lounge, inviting Adrianna to sit down on one of the large sofas that dominated the room. He then asked if he could get them a drink.

Simon gave his father a puzzled look.

"Where's mother, dad?" he asked, concerned. "I've never known her not to be here to greet me when I come for the weekend. Is she OK?"

His father sighed.

"She's absolutely fine, son. She was upset at not being able to welcome your young lady herself, but I'm afraid we've had a bit of a scare. Just after you phoned tonight we received a call from your aunt Devina to say that Jack has been rushed into hospital after a suspected heart attack. You know how emotional your mother's sister gets, although in this case it's understandable. Your mother was unable to get any coherent details from Devina, so she decided to go straight to the hospital to find out what's happening and to calm her down. The last thing Jack needs at the moment is to be worrying about her.

"She's hoping to join us later this evening, but you know what hospitals are like. They never tell you anything in a hurry, so I'm afraid we may be on our own for dinner. She's going to phone when she has any news. Anna is also away visiting one of her relatives this weekend, so your mother has cooked a casserole. It just needs heating up and I'm sure I can manage the vegetables – I'm not yet entirely useless."

He laughed to himself, coughed slightly and shuffled off to get the drinks and heat up the oven.

Simon sat down beside Adrianna and, taking advantage of his father's absence from the room, kissed her warmly.

"I've looked forward to this weekend so much," he whispered in her ear, caressing her neck. "I hope you won't be too bored with my parents' company. I promise we'll do something on our own tomorrow, just the two of us. There's so much I want to show you."

Adrianna released herself from his arms, which were holding her close. She needed to get Daniel Feldman into his office on his own and Simon was a nuisance. She smiled apologetically at Simon, who was now pulling a disappointed face, and tried to keep calm.

"I'm sorry, *caro*," she purred at him. "It does not feel right to display such affection in your parents' home before they have had time to get to know me, or I them. I do not feel it is polite."

She stroked the side of his face briefly with her hand and moved away from him, sitting up straight as she did so. Checking that her hair was in place, she then ran her hands over her skirt to remove any creases. Simon laughed at her sudden primness, dismissing it as some kind of Italian custom.

As he was about to tease her, his father came back into the room carrying a tray holding two glasses of wine and a Scotch. He handed a glass to Adrianna, and as she took a sip, she discreetly looked at the clock on the mantelpiece. It was gone seven-thirty. She had to act fast before things became too difficult to control.

"Simon tells me your mother is Italian," she said to Daniel with a smile. "Do you have any photographs of her and your Italian family? I would really like to see them. I love England, but Italy will always be my home and closest to my heart."

She fluttered her eyelashes at Daniel, desperately hoping that he kept his photo album in his office. She was not disappointed and Daniel was more than happy to take the bait.

"As a matter of fact Adrianna, I do," he replied, with a twinkle in his eye. "I have an album in my office. I'll go and get it. Simon can explain the photos to you while I finish off the dinner."

He got up and went into the hall, and was about to open the door to the office when the telephone rang. Adrianna felt her frustration build as she heard him answer the phone.

"Darling," he exclaimed, on recognising his wife's voice. "How's Jack? Have they told you anything yet?"

The answer was obviously good news, though not entirely what Daniel was expecting to hear. "Oh, OK darling," he replied, a hint of disappointment in his voice. "Yes of course, don't worry. Simon and Adrianna are here and I have everything under control. I'm glad Jack is going to be fine. Give him our love and we'll see you later. Take care driving home, dear. Bye."

He replaced the receiver and came back into the lounge. Adrianna felt a wave of panic rise inside her and looked at the clock again. It was almost a quarter to eight.

"That was your mother," he told Simon. "Uncle Jack did have a heart attack, but they managed to get him to the hospital before any lasting damage could be done to his heart. He's had emergency coronary angioplasty surgery and they've inserted a stent. He's going to be fine. Your mother is taking Devina home, but feels she ought to stay with her for a while, to make sure she's OK. She said she'd grab a bite to eat at Devina's, so it's going to be just us three for dinner."

Simon felt sorry for his father, knowing how much he relied on his mother to act as hostess on these occasions.

"It's OK dad," he replied, trying to reassure him. "I'm glad uncle Jack is going to be fine and I'm sorry mother isn't here to welcome Adrianna. However, it'll be nice to spend some time talking to you, without mother dominating the conversation. She means well, but she can sometimes monopolise things. There's going to be plenty of time over the weekend for her and Adrianna to get to know each other. We're here until Monday morning."

Daniel chuckled at this description of his wife and, feeling a little guilty for agreeing with his son, started to walk towards his chair again. Adrianna, who was now becoming desperate, stopped him midway.

"You were going to show me your photographs, Signor Feldman," she spluttered, almost giving away her panic."

Daniel turned towards her, remembering his original mission.

"Of course I was, my dear," he replied, smiling. "My wife totally made me forget my quest. I'll get them now."

Adrianna smiled wanly back at him, feeling the relief engulf her as he went back out into the hall and opened the office door.

CHAPTER 36

Mark watched from his hiding place as the man disappeared through the French windows. He had no idea who he was, but it did not need rocket science to work out that he had not made an appointment.

Following an overcast day, it was already beginning to get dark, so it was easier to move around the garden without being conspicuous. He used whatever cover of shrubbery he could to get as close as possible to the window and then, keeping his back tightly against the wall of the house, he slid cagily towards the edge of the window frame and carefully peered through the glass.

It was too dark to make out where the man had gone, but Mark's instincts told him that he was probably still lingering in the room. This was not at all how he had planned things. What the hell was going on? How many more people were going to turn up tonight, for God's sake?

As his eyes adjusted, he became aware of a slight movement in the room, but it did not look as if the intruder was searching around or trying to rob the place. He seemed to be waiting for something… or someone.

At that moment, the office door opened and the light came on. Mark was now able to clearly see the intruder standing behind the door. His concern heightened when he caught sight of the gun in his right hand.

As the man he could only assume was Daniel Feldman came into the room he was immediately grabbed from behind. A hand was placed firmly over his mouth, while the gun was jabbed against his temple. The younger man was strong and it was obvious to Mark that the older man was not.

With the light now on in the room, Mark was virtually invisible against the dark, unlit garden. He stood back against the wall, trying to think what he should do. Apart from anything, this guy was stealing his thunder. The French window was slightly ajar where the young man had not quite shut it properly, so Mark could hear their conversation.

"Don't make a sound, Signor Feldman," the gun-toting man hissed into Daniel's ear. "You and I have unfinished business, and we wouldn't want to be disturbed now, would we?"

Daniel started to wheeze and pointed at the inhaler on his desk. His assailant followed the direction of his finger and, dragging Daniel with him, moved towards the desk. When he saw the object to which Daniel was frantically gesticulating he smiled to himself.

"Well, well," he remarked, realising what it was. "*You* appear to be the weak man now I see. Even better."

He spun Daniel round and forced him onto a chair by the desk, keeping the gun pressed against his temple, but removing his hand from Daniel's mouth.

"What do you want?" asked Daniel, trying to control his breathing. "I'm a sick man, but I can give you money, if that's what you're after. Just tell me how much you want."

The young man sneered at him.

"Your money is of no use today, old man. You are twenty-six years too late with your offer," he sneered as Simon appeared at the door, closely followed by Adrianna.

"Dad, what's keeping you? The photos can…. "

Simon stopped mid-sentence as his brain registered the scene in front of him.

"What the bloody hell do you think you're doing?" he exclaimed, as his father began to cough. "Leave my father alone for God's sake, he's a sick man. He has emphysema."

Spinning round, the Italian glared icily at Simon, pushing the gun harder against Daniel's head, while at the same time slipping his arm around his throat and forcing his head backwards. Simon made an involuntary move forward but a clicking sound close to his ear stopped him in his tracks. He swivelled his head to find himself staring at the barrel of a gun, held by Adrianna, who was also glaring at him.

"My God, Adrianna," he cried. "What are you doing? I don't understand. What's this all about?"

Adrianna continued to glare at him, her eyes filled with hatred.

"Revenge, *caro*," she stated coldly. "Do you really think I would stoop so low as to allow myself to be picked up in a bar by a pathetic, drunken Englishman? You Feldman men are so arrogant."

She spat out the last sentence with utter contempt, almost shaking with anger. Simon, finding it hard to comprehend what he was hearing, turned his head back and forth between the two of them, desperately seeking an explanation.

"I don't expect *stronzos* like you and this piece of filth to remember everyone they have left to suffer, just to satisfy their greed for money and power," the man growled. "But I'm here to make sure your father remembers one very important person before I send him to beg forgiveness before God.

"It's time you found out the truth about your beloved father."

From his concealed position outside the window, Mark silently watched events inside unfold.

The situation had taken a serious turn for the worst. He had been thinking of rushing the young man from behind, using the element of surprise that he undoubtedly possessed. However, now that there were two gun-wielding protagonists, ideas of heroism had disappeared as his mind frantically tried to process what was going on.

While Mark contemplated his next move, Chris and Tim, who had needed Tim's Sat Nav to guide them through the traffic, finally arrived. They parked behind Mark's car.

"That's Simon's car," Chris said, spotting it on the drive. "They're here already, and so is Mark. We may be too late."

"Not necessarily," replied Tim, scouring the darkening garden with his eyes. "He told me that he was going to get a feel for the situation first, to make sure that Feldman and his wife were both at home before making his move. Let's see if we can do the same. It's almost dark now and the street lighting isn't that brilliant. We should have enough cover to sneak around the building and see if we can see any signs of life inside. Hopefully, they don't pull their curtains with all this space around the house. Come on, follow me."

They got out of the car, crossed the road and slipped quietly into the garden. There was a light on in the hallway, but the rooms at the front of the house were in darkness. Tim decided to check out the rear of the house, indicating for Chris to follow him. Together, they carefully picked their way through the shrubs to the back garden. They could see lights coming from two of the rooms and a dark figure leaning against the wall, adjacent to the French windows. From where they were standing they could not identify the shadowy figure, but Chris prayed it was Mark.

They tiptoed towards him, conscious that they did not want to startle him into making a sudden sound or movement.

Meanwhile, Adrianna had forced Simon to sit and, finding some tape in one of the desk drawers, had bound his hands behind him, securing them to the back of the chair. She bound his legs to the legs of the chair for good measure. He continued to demand an explanation until she grew tired of his protestations and angrily slapped tape across his mouth. This did little to calm his agitation until she pressed her gun against his temple, threatening to shoot him if he did not calm down and stay still.

Tim softly whispered Mark's name, trying to keep the shock element to a minimum. On hearing Tim's voice, Mark started, but as he did so Tim's hand wrapped itself around his mouth and pulled him away from the window before he could give the game away.

"Bloody hell Tim, you scared the living daylights out of me. What are you doing here?" spluttered Mark in a harsh whisper that betrayed both shock and relief. "For God's sake keep your voice down, as they might hear you through the French windows."

He pointed to the slightly open window as Chris peered around Tim's shoulder. Mark hit his forehead in exasperation.

"Not you too. What is this, a reunion?"

"We wanted to warn you," replied Tim quietly, glaring at him. "We knew you hadn't bargained for Simon turning up, especially with a partner. We wanted to stop you before you did something you'd regret. Things could have turned very ugly."

"The boat's already sailed on that one I'm afraid," Mark replied sarcastically, checking the room to make sure they had not been heard. Nothing seemed to have changed. "Someone else seems to have a desperate desire to talk to Feldman, only he appears to need a gun to do it."

Tim was about to ask Mark what on Earth he was talking about, but decided to take a look for himself. He slid along the wall to the window and cautiously peered through the glass. After a quick scan of the room to assess the situation, he slid back and faced the others.

"Perhaps we should come back later," he said sheepishly, grabbing hold of Chris's arm and starting to pull her away.

"We can't leave them like this," snapped Mark, stopping Tim in his tracks. "What if it was one of us in there?"

Now that he was no longer on his own, a plan had started to form in his mind.

"OK," he whispered to Chris. "Now that you're here, this is what's going to happen.

"The situation seems to be a bit more serious than I originally thought," he continued with masterly understatement, "and it looks like we're going to need backup. Go back to the car and phone the police. Tell them it's a hostage situation and that guns are involved. That should get them off their backsides. Tell them you've heard screaming, and make sure you sound really scared to stress the urgency – we don't want some plod on a push bike!"

Chris made a face, and was about to protest when it clicked that a scared woman might have more effect on a switchboard receptionist than a scared man. She reluctantly made her way back to the road, but not before insisting that he be careful and not do anything stupid.

"Right," Mark continued, turning to Tim. "Your turn. You need to create a diversion so that the woman leaves the room. I can't tackle two of them, not when they're both armed. Go around to the back door and make some noise in the kitchen. We'll have to hope they haven't locked the door for the night. I don't think there's anyone else in the house or they would have heard the shouting by now and come to investigate."

Tim hesitated for a moment, action hero not having been one of his chosen career paths.

"She has a gun, in case you've forgotten," he pointed out. "What am I supposed to do? Casually ask if I can borrow it for a moment?"

Mark had come up with some wild ideas over the years, but this one topped the lot, he thought with a mixture of trepidation and disbelief.

"Use your imagination, dummy," snapped Mark. "You'll obviously have to surprise her so that you can disarm her. She's a woman, not a sumo wrestler! I'm the one who's drawn the short straw here. Matey in there obviously knows how to handle himself. Now stop whining and get on with it. We might not have much time."

Tim realised he did not have much choice and with a last snort of indignation turned towards the back door. But before leaving, he turned back and glared at Mark.

"By the way, Superman, Chris knows everything," he said smugly. "She made me tell her, so you're going to have a lot of explaining to do later – if that guy in there doesn't get to you first that is."

With that he disappeared into the darkness.

CHAPTER 37

The Italian had been gradually losing his temper with the younger Feldman. He wanted full attention for the grand finale. However, he felt calmer and back in control of things now that Adrianna had silenced him. He tightened his grip on Daniel – who was terrified, wheezing and breathless – and smiled sadistically at Simon.

"Tell me, Signor Daniel Feldman," he sneered into Daniel's ear, still looking at Simon. "Do you remember your old friend, Roberto de Luca? The friend you grew up with? The friend who was always there for you when you were staying with your grandparents... back in Italy? Who always spoke up for you when you were in trouble with your parents? Whose family supported your father when he first started his business, despite the poverty that had been inflicted on them after the war?"

He felt Daniel grow tense under the grip of his arm as the old man began to cast his mind back.

"He would have done anything for you, but you virtually spat in his face when he needed you the most."

As the vivid memory began to manifest itself in his mind, the rage grew even stronger. Struggling to control his emotions, he remembered his father's last words: "You are an Italian and Italian men are brave." He took a deep breath.

"He only needed 23 million lire," he continued. "An impossible sum to him, but nothing to you. He was desperate, but after all he had done to help you, you refused him and left him to his fate. Like kicking a stray dog while he was down."

Daniel was by now shaking as memories came flooding back to him.

"He was a gambler," he panted. "If I had given him the money he would only have gambled it away again. I wanted him to realise the responsibility he had to Isabella and also to his children. He was tearing her apart. She didn't deserve that."

He could only get the words out slowly and indistinctly, coughing, sweating and struggling for breath. No effort of will power could prevent the tears welling up in his eyes.

The Italian was unmoved.

"But still you didn't bother to find out who was calling in the debt, or what was going to happen to him if he did not pay up, did you?" he hissed. "Well let me enlighten you, *signor*. He owed the money to Signor Rizzo. I'm sure your father knew Rizzo only too well. Anyone who had business in Tuscany at that time knew Rizzo. He controlled everyone of importance in the area, including the chief of police. He had contacts everywhere. He wasn't a man known for his compassion or for his forgiving nature. Anyone owing him money was right to be scared."

Daniel vividly remembered the last time he had spoken to Roberto, and how scared he had been. He thought it was because he was afraid that Isabella would find out he was still gambling after promising her, on his life, that he had stopped. Having a soft spot for Isabella, Daniel had considered it a salutary lesson for a man who deceived his wife with such apparent ease and lack of conscience. It had not occurred to him at the time that leaving the debt unsettled could have such a fatal consequence.

"I'm sorry I didn't help him," he sobbed, his wheezing turning to a cough again. "I really thought it was just another of his regular gambling debts. He only ever played with the locals and the debts were usually small enough to meet. When he asked for such a large sum I thought he was trying it on, thinking I was a soft touch. It was only later that I heard who he was mixed up with and how serious things were, but I was back in London by then and it was impossible to rectify the situation or turn back the clock."

The gunman lowered his voice to a threatening murmur.

"Oh, it was certainly serious, Signor Feldman. He was murdered... and you could have saved him."

He waited while Daniel absorbed those words.

"I think it's time I introduced myself," he continued. "I am Roberto's son, Giovanni de Luca and this is my sister, Adrianna. I was only five years old when, due to your ambivalence, they came for him and beat him to death, right in front of my mother. They gave us only days to leave our home and everything we owned before they came back to claim it as forfeit for the debt, leaving my mother destitute with two small children to care for.

"Fortunately, a neighbour was kind enough to take us in. My

mother, however, never recovered from my father's death, and she *never* let us forget that it was our duty to avenge him. Signor Rizzo and the gorillas he called sons have already paid for their crimes, now it's your turn."

* * * * * *

Tim had reached the kitchen and was now cautiously looking through the window to make sure the room was empty. Relieved that it was, he carefully tried the door handle and slipped inside. "So far so good," he thought.

The door to the hall was ajar, so, quietly closing the back door behind him, he tiptoed over to it and listened to assure himself that he had not been heard. It was a long hallway and the kitchen was quite a distance from the office, so he could only just hear a man's voice rising in anger. It was enough, however, to realise that he had to act fast.

Looking around his eyes first descended on the saucepans on the cooker. They were full of vegetables and water, so he dismissed them as too clumsy to use. He picked a frying pan up, weighing it in his hands and calculating its potential effectiveness as a club. It was reassuringly heavy so he settled on it as his weapon of choice.

Returning to the back door, Tim opened it and banged it shut again. He ran to the other door and hid behind it, praying it would be the girl, rather than the guy, who came to investigate.

The noise of the back door banging had the desired effect. Both Giovanni and Adrianna looked towards the office door, and then at each other.

"Must be the old woman," snapped Giovanni. "Go and deal with her before she realises what's happening."

Adrianna nodded and, after taking a quick look at Simon's bonds to make sure he was securely tied, left the room and walked purposefully towards the kitchen.

From his position behind the door, Tim heard her footsteps. Taking a deep breath he steadied himself and raised the frying pan in readiness. The door was pushed open and Adrianna entered the room, holding her gun in front of her. Tim waited until she was past him and about to turn in his direction. He swung the frying pan with as much force as he could muster, hitting her arm and sending the gun flying across the room, where it came to rest under the kitchen table. Dropping the pan, he grabbed Adrianna from behind as she doubled up in pain, cradling her arm. He threw his hand over her mouth to stifle her cries. She tried to wriggle free and bite his fingers but Tim was stronger and heavier and had his other arm wrapped around her in a vice-like grip.

"Struggle and I'll really hurt you," he whispered into her ear. He could hear her muffled curses through his hand as she thrashed around. She was obviously not going to give up easily, so he forced her to lie face down on the floor. He straddled her back, pinning her arms with his legs, while keeping his hand over her mouth.

Adrianna continued to writhe so he reached up with his free hand and grabbed a tea towel hanging from a cupboard handle. He forced the towel into her mouth and tied the ends behind her head. Spotting a laundry basket nearby with some clothes in it ready for the wash, he squeezed his thighs against Adrianna's arms and body to prevent her from moving and reached over towards it. Grabbing the basket, he pulled it towards him. Inside he found two pairs of thick tights, and using his weight and strength he managed to bind the arms and legs of his furious captive.

Now that she was fully restrained and unable to cause him any physical harm, he pulled her up and, supporting her around her waist, dragged her over to one of the kitchen chairs. Forcing her to sit down, he adjusted the tights until she was bound tightly to the chair. She glared at him, still trying to free herself. He ignored her and reached under the kitchen table to retrieve the gun.

"Now," he whispered. "You're going to be a good girl and sit there quietly, aren't you? Your friend is about to receive a visitor and we wouldn't want to spoil the surprise, would we?"

He pulled up another chair, straddling it to face her and pointed the gun at her head.

CHAPTER 38

Mark watched Adrianna leave the room. One down and one to go, he hoped. Chris should have alerted the police by now, but he could not wait for them to put in an appearance.

He once more surveyed the scene before him, making a mental note of where everyone was in the room. Daniel Feldman was seated in a chair to one side of his desk, facing the office door. The intruder was standing directly behind him with his back to the window, threatening him with a gun. Simon was a few feet in front of them, tied to a chair. Mark only had one chance of grabbing the gun before he too would be in the firing line. Timing was of the essence.

The man was becoming increasingly agitated, as he waited for the woman to return. In fact, Giovanni had heard a faint cry coming from the kitchen but was not sure whether it was from the wife or Adrianna. Mark heard him shout out to her.

"Adrianna, what's going on? Get back in here and bring the old woman with you."

Her prolonged absence was obviously unnerving him, so Mark

decided now was his time.

Bending down and picking up a stone from the ground, he gently and quietly pulled open the French window. He put his finger to his lips, indicating to Simon, who saw him appear at the window, not to react. Bemused, Simon readily obliged, and quickly returned his gaze to his father, in order not to arouse any suspicion.

Mark threw the stone over into the opposite corner of the room. On hearing the stone resounding on the wooden floor, Giovanni instinctively turned to see what it was, momentarily relaxing his grip on Daniel. Mark rushed him, throwing an arm around his throat and grabbing the hand that held the gun. Taken by surprise, Giovanni completely let go of Daniel, allowing himself to be pulled backwards. Mark swung him around and crashed his hand down onto the desk. The force of the blow knocked the gun out of Giovanni's hand, but not before it went off and sent a bullet whistling past Daniel's ear. The gun spun across the desktop and landed on the floor by the window.

Alarmed by the proximity of the bullet, Daniel instinctively threw himself to the floor, taking cover behind the desk. Seeing the two men grappling with each other, he made use of his sudden release and started to crawl across the floor towards Simon, but his erratic breathing forced him to stop half way.

Finally reacting to the situation, Giovanni brought his elbow back and slammed it hard into Mark's ribs, sending him staggering backwards. This gave Giovanni time to swing round and land a hefty punch squarely on Mark's jaw. Mark fell to the ground, but as Giovanni advanced, he had his legs kicked away from him, knocking him off balance and sending him crashing to the floor. Jumping up, Mark threw himself on top of Giovanni, pinning him to the floor, and returned the punch… twice. Giovanni, however, was stronger than Mark had anticipated, and putting both his hands on Mark's chest, forced him to one side, before jumping up and landing a forceful kick into Mark's stomach. With Mark doubled up in pain, temporarily winded, Giovanni rushed to the window and picked up his gun.

"I don't know who you are, *signor*, but that was a very foolish mistake," he screamed at Mark, aiming the gun at him. "For that you will share the fate of Signor Feldman."

He started to put pressure on the trigger, but as he was about to shoot, something hard came crashing down on his head. Stunned, he staggered forward.

In what seemed like slow motion, the gun slowly slid out of his hand and he slumped to the floor, unconscious amid the remnants of a ceramic flowerpot, the contents of which were now scattered all around him.

Behind him stood a trembling Chris.

Tim had heard the commotion, and rushing from the kitchen towards the office, he was just in time to see Giovanni crumple to the floor. It took him a second or two to grasp what had happened but then, stooping down, he checked Giovanni's pulse to make sure he was alive. He was, but out cold and his head was bleeding profusely.

"He was going to shoot Mark," spluttered Chris, walking into the room and glaring down at Giovanni.

Realising that everyone was looking at her, she blushed and turned towards Daniel Feldman, who was staring at her from the floor, mouth wide open. He had just processed who the first two intruders were, now he had a new set to get to grips with.

"I'm sorry about the plant," Chris apologised, trying to salvage what was left of Mrs Feldman's pride and joy. "The flowerpot was all I could find that was heavy enough. I *will* replace them though."

She gave him an apologetic smile.

Daniel Feldman, slowly dragging himself off the floor and into an upright position, began to laugh – more in hysterical reaction to the dramatic events of the evening than amusement at Chris' prosaic concern for the welfare of his wife's plant.

"Damn the plant, my dear," he chuckled. "You appear to have saved all our skins, whoever you are. Although this young man was making a fair fist of it."

He transferred his gaze towards Mark, who had by now pulled himself back onto his feet and hobbled over to Simon, where he was engaged in releasing him from his bondage.

As soon as Simon was free of his gag his thoughts immediately went to Adrianna.

"Where's Adrianna?" he asked, looking at Tim and noticing the gun in his hand. He was desperately clinging to the hope that her violent reaction to him was the result of some coercion or threat to her. "What have you done with her? Is she alright?"

Tim stood up from where he was crouched over Giovanni.

"She's fine," he replied. "Although she's a bit tied up at the moment. She's a bit of a spitfire, isn't she? And stronger than she looks – put up quite a fight."

They were interrupted by the sound of a wailing siren, which filled the room as an Armed Response Vehicle raced down the road and screeched to a halt outside the house. Three Specialist Firearms Officers from the Surrey Police Tactical Firearms Unit, dressed in bulletproof vests and holding Glock 17s, took up their positions behind the shrubs on the lawn. A voice emanating from a loud hailer announced that there were armed officers on the premises and they were fully prepared to use their weapons if necessary.

Daniel walked over to his desk and picked up his inhaler. After taking a deep breath from it, he slowly made his way over to the window and held up his hand to the men outside.

"It's OK officers," he called out to the men on the lawn. "The danger appears to be over now, but I'd be grateful if you would kindly remove this uninvited thug and his accomplice from my house. They have definitely outstayed their welcome."

He turned his head back towards the others and smiled reassuringly.

One of the officers emerged from the darkness of the garden and stepped carefully into the room, warily holding his gun in front of him. His two colleagues immediately followed behind him. They surveyed the room before resting their eyes on the prostrate Giovanni, who was groaning as he slowly started to regain consciousness. Tim was still holding Adrianna's gun, and all three officers instinctively pointed their weapons at him. It dawned on Tim that he was a suspect, but Daniel intervened.

"No, this young man came to my rescue," he informed the officers, pointing at Tim.

"The other one is in the kitchen," Tim nervously blurted. "This is her gun, officer."

He handed the gun, butt first, to the first officer, who was still eyeing him suspiciously, and then indicated the way to the kitchen. The officer followed him out, his gun still at the ready, leaving his colleagues to deal with Giovanni.

"We'll need to take initial statements from all of you tonight, sir," remarked one of the remaining officers to Daniel, as, after checking the extent of his wound, they hauled Giovanni off the floor and forced his arms behind his back. "But it would help us if you could either come down to the station this evening or tomorrow morning, at the latest, to give more formal ones. We also need to seal off this room for the time being. The forensic team are on their way. They'll need to take everyone's fingerprints. In the meantime, could you all move to another room please?"

Daniel nodded in acknowledgement.

"My wife is not here at the moment and will be worried about me," he said. "If you don't mind, I'd rather wait until she gets home. It's been a traumatic experience for all of us. Perhaps it would be better all round if we could give our statements in the morning, if that's OK."

The officer agreed and told Daniel that, if they needed any further information, someone would contact him.

Daniel thanked them and walked over to Simon, to check that he was OK, while the two officers marched Giovanni towards the open French windows. Just before the three of them disappeared into the darkness, Giovanni twisted his head towards Daniel.

"This is not over, Signor Feldman," he snarled. "Tonight you were lucky. Next time you won't be."

The officers dragged him away, leaving Daniel staring thoughtfully after him.

Adrianna appeared at the door, her arms held firmly behind her back by the officer who had gone to fetch her.

"Adriana," cried Simon, jumping up as soon as he saw her, desperately searching her face for some sign of reassurance. "I can't believe this is happening. Tell me it's all a mistake. You know how much you mean to me. I don't understand how you could do this after we've become so close. I thought you loved me."

Adrianna stared at him coldly.

"Love you, Simon?" she snarled in reply, narrowing her eyes and giving a hollow laugh. "How could I possibly love someone whose family was responsible for my father's death? Every moment I spent with you made my flesh crawl. I will never feel clean again. God will punish you. I hope you rot in hell."

She spat at him, before being hauled away by the officer. Simon watched her go, his face betraying how deeply her words had pierced him. Daniel gently put his hand on his son's shoulder.

After the police had taken statements from everyone, sealed off the office and finally driven away with their charges, the forensic team arrived to carry out their work. Having given them everything they needed, Daniel focussed his attention on the strangers now assembled in his lounge.

"Well," he declared. "Maybe now I'll get to know who my unexpected, but welcome, visitors are?"

He looked at Simon and raised a questioning eyebrow. Simon, still in shock, pointed first at Chris.

"This is Christina Newman, dad. She's my assistant. And this is our receptionist, Tim," he said, pointing at Tim, "As for Action Man here, I have no idea who he is. You'll have to ask him. I don't understand or know anything anymore."

He sat down, lent forward and put his head in his hands. Daniel stroked his son's head.

Mark dusted himself down and holding his arm across his stomach, which was now beginning to throb, he turned to face Daniel.

"I hadn't intended for things to happen in quite such dramatic fashion as this," he began, raising his eyebrows. "I had planned to be a little more composed for our first meeting. Still, here goes."

He shot a glance at Chris, who was displaying absolutely no signs of being surprised. In fact she now raised her eyebrows at him. Tim had been telling the truth – she did know everything.

"You may not know who *I* am," he continued, "but you certainly knew someone very close to me. Her name is Sally Dempster. Apparently, you knew her extremely well."

He paused to see the name register with Daniel, before resuming his monologue.

"She was your personal assistant back in 1984, very personal apparently. So personal that as a result she became pregnant, at which point you decided that her services were no longer required and dismissed her. Not very gentlemanly conduct was it, Mr Feldman?"

Daniel began to look decidedly uncomfortable as the significance of what Mark was saying dawned on him. He dropped his hand from

Simon's head and gripped the back of his armchair to steady himself, while continuing to stare at Mark in silence. He started to shake and breathe heavily.

"It took me a long time to realise the truth and, when I did, set about finding you," continued Mark, a feeling of satisfaction rising inside him as Daniel's face showed the impact of his revelations.

"For reasons that are beyond me, she kept quiet about everything, only confiding in her best friend. The friend, however, wasn't as careful. Too much alcohol at a party and a few careless words were enough to raise suspicions in my mind. I tried to press her further, but, realising that she had said too much already, caution got the better of the alcohol and she clammed up. I was left to gradually put the pieces together by myself. So, now that I have finally found you, allow me to introduce myself. I'm Mark Dempster."

Daniel swallowed hard before answering.

"Then you must be…."

Mark interrupted him.

"Yes, that's right. Hello *dad*!"

CHAPTER 39

Silence descended upon the room while Mark's declaration took effect. Daniel continued to stare at Mark, his mouth agape. Chris and Tim exchanged glances, unsure of what to do next.

It was Simon who broke the silence.

"Would someone like to tell me what the hell is going on here?" he asked plaintively. "Because I'm having real difficulty in comprehending any of it. Who is this, dad? And what does he mean *hello dad*? Is this some kind of a joke, because I seem to have lost my sense of humour?"

He looked at his father in sheer bewilderment.

Daniel averted his gaze from Mark and turned to confront his son.

"I'm so sorry, Simon," he said quietly, wheezing slightly. "I told you, the day we had lunch together, that I had done things in my past of which I was not particularly proud. I didn't expect you to find out about them like this. Failing to help Roberto de Luca was just one of them. My part in the treatment of Sally Dempster was another. Simon, this is Mark…. your half brother."

234

Simon transferred his gaze from his father to Mark and then returned it to his father again, trying and failing to take in what he was hearing. In just a few short moments his whole life had come apart at the seams. First, his girlfriend had turned out to be a revenge-seeking potential assassin and now his father seemed a stranger to him. To cap it all he had suddenly acquired a brother, at least half of one.

"How is this possible?" he finally asked. "All these years and not a word about a brother. Why was it kept from me? How come no one in the family has ever mentioned anything to do with this? I think you owe me an explanation, especially after forcing me to abandon any plans I might have had for my future, because, as your *only* child, I had a duty to carry on the business. Oh, and let's not forget that hypocritical lecture I got a few weeks ago about not getting too involved with the staff. So, go on dad… enlighten me!"

He was beginning to shake with anger, aimed not only at his father but also at himself for not standing up to him earlier.

Daniel briefly closed his eyes to gather his thoughts, and then looked around the room at the others. Everyone was staring at him in anticipation.

"I think both of you deserve to hear the whole truth and not just a brief interpretation of it," he replied, addressing both of his sons. "It's the least I can do. Let's all make ourselves comfortable, and I promise that I *will* tell you anything and everything you want to know."

* * * * * *

Once everyone was settled on one or other of the two sofas in the lounge, and he was seated in front of them in his armchair, Daniel, having now gained control of his breathing, embarked on his explanation.

"That day by the river, Simon," he began, "I also told you that your grandfather was not a particularly kind man. He would always put the business first, whether it was to the detriment of friends or not. Well, that included his dealings with me. As his son I was a valuable part of his plan for the future and nothing would interfere with that, as far as he was concerned."

He paused as he cast his mind back to the days of his youth. So many memories had been forced back to haunt him this evening that his words became hard to deliver.

"I was very much like you, Simon, as a young man," he continued, smiling to himself. "I had an eye for the ladies and, like most young men in their early twenties, I revelled in the attention that I received from women. Looking back, though, I now realise that it was my wealth and privileged position that was a major part of the attraction. I certainly had no intentions of settling down and getting married in the foreseeable future. My father, however, had other ideas."

He got up, went over to the drinks cabinet, took out a bottle of Scotch and poured himself a large one.

"Would anyone else care to join me?" he asked. Everyone declined except Simon, who suddenly felt the need for alcoholic support. Pouring out another Scotch, Daniel handed the glass to him before returning to his seat.

"My father had a good friend, who ran a similar kind of business,

236

but with better links abroad," resumed Daniel, taking a slug from his tumbler. "Michael Chapman. He had two daughters, the eldest, Caroline, was your mother," he said, looking at Simon, who was staring blankly into his drink. "My father, with the full agreement of her father, decided that it would be in the interest of both families if she and I got married and thereby consolidate the two businesses. This would give both he and Michael the potential to take on bigger clients in more countries. Michael had contacts in several European countries, but not in Italy, which was where my father would prove valuable.

"This proposal pleased everyone… except me. However, I was given no choice in the matter and it was a done deal before I even had a chance to speak to Caroline. To be fair, she felt the same about marrying me but neither of us felt able to refuse. We had both been brought up not to challenge the authority of our fathers. So, we reluctantly complied with their wishes."

At the mention of his parents' marriage, Simon jerked his head up and glared at Daniel, an alarming thought suddenly striking him.

"Mother, oh my God!" he cried. "Does she know about all this, or have you kept her in the dark as well?"

Daniel looked at him reassuringly.

"Yes, Simon," he replied. "She knows all about Mark. Has done for years, but I'll come to that."

He took another calming sip of his Scotch.

"Your mother and I made the best of things," he continued. "Neither of us was in love with the other, although we were genuinely fond of each other, as our families had been close friends for years. I tried hard to be a good husband and she was every bit the dutiful, albeit resigned, wife. Two years later you were born and I felt the proudest man alive. However, your mother suffered complications and, as a result, she had to have a hysterectomy, ruling out the chance of any more children. She was devastated and, for over a year, she withdrew into herself, hardly speaking to me at all, preferring to devote all her attentions towards you. It was a painful time for both of us, but we tried hard not to let it affect you. We both loved you so much."

He paused again, staring into his glass before draining its contents.

Simon felt a lump in his throat. He swallowed hard, trying not to let signs of emotion give him away and give Daniel an excuse for leaving anything out.

"It was around that time that Sally came to work for me," Daniel pressed on, this time looking towards Mark, who had sat the whole time with his head bowed, trying to avoid looking at Simon. Despite his anger towards Daniel, he also felt unexpected compassion towards his newly acquired brother, who until barely an hour ago had been totally unaware that he was not an only child. Daniel had treated them both badly. They at least had that much in common.

"She was young, beautiful and full of life, as well as being extremely good at her job," said Daniel, smiling at Mark. "We got on really well together, and I soon found myself wanting to spend all of my time with her, rather than being at home. I began to work late, making all sorts of excuses for Sally to work late as well, just to be with her as much as possible. I even engineered trips to our overseas offices so that we could be away together. Then one day we both realised that we'd fallen in love with each other. She was like a breath of fresh air and it wasn't long before the inevitable happened and she fell pregnant… with you, Mark."

At this, Mark suddenly looked up at Daniel.

"I think I'll have that drink now, if you don't mind," he said, betraying no emotion at all. Daniel smiled at him, got up and went over to the drinks cabinet where he poured out a Scotch for Mark, and another one for himself.

"You'd better make that three," exclaimed Simon, holding out his glass. "It looks as if tonight is going to be rather long and tortuous."

Daniel raised an eyebrow and, nodding in agreement, took Simon's glass and refilled it. He returned to his seat, where he sat cradling his own glass for at least a couple of minutes.

"I really did love your mother, Mark," he resumed at last. "But when my father found out about the affair, and especially the impending arrival of a child, he was furious, accusing me of irresponsibility and threatening me with all sorts of reprisals. He was not about to let any weakness on my part jeopardise his newly acquired empire or his position within it. He ordered me to break off all communications with Sally, concentrate on my wife and child, and to think about the family and the business. I was still young and, quite frankly, scared of my father. He would stop at nothing to protect his own interests and I was worried that my refusal might cause him to be vindictive towards Sally."

Mark now had his eyes firmly fixed on Daniel.

"You were worried you'd lose everything you mean," he snapped. "If you loved my mother as much as you say you did, you'd have found a way to be with her. Be honest, you were more in love with your lifestyle and afraid your father would cut you off without a penny, weren't you?"

Daniel gradually lifted his gaze from his glass to look Mark in the eyes.

"I'm not proud of my behaviour, Mark," he said quietly, "but you have to understand things were different then. A father's word was law, and I was brought up to know where my duty lay. I already had a wife and young child to think of, and it wasn't their fault that I had been weak and neglected my responsibilities. It wasn't Sally's fault either, as it was me who pursued her. The whole thing was a mess, and I suppose I took the coward's way out. I obeyed my father and let him deal with the situation."

Mark's eyes darkened.

"What do you mean, deal with the situation?" he demanded, his voice quivering. "Was that all my mother and I had become to you – a situation?"

"No Mark, it broke my heart to leave her," replied Daniel softly. "The look on her face when I told her that, not only could we never see each other again, but that she was going to lose the job she loved so much is something that will stay with me forever."

He covered his eyes with his hand, sliding it slowly down his face before continuing, struggling to hold back the tears.

"My father decided that, despite the circumstances, you were still his grandchild. However, he couldn't openly acknowledge you without causing offence to his friend Michael, Caroline's father. After all, Simon was Michael's grandchild too. So, he did the next best thing, by his way of thinking. He made a deal with Sally. He would pay for your education in order that you would have a good start in life, one befitting a Feldman. Then, on your twenty-fifth birthday, he would settle a lump sum of £250,000 on you. In return, your mother was never to reveal your father's name, or where the money was coming from, to anyone... especially to you. She was also never to try and contact the family again, except through their solicitor, who had been instructed to make sure that all the financial details were adhered to and that you wanted for nothing."

"Except a father!" corrected Mark, finishing his drink and, putting the glass on the coffee table in front of him. He leant back on the sofa. "Well, at least that explains my generous, so-called inheritance!"

He glared at Daniel.

"OK, now that I've heard your side of the story, would you like to hear how *my* life panned out, after having been set up so generously?" he asked, sarcastically. "Well, *granddaddy* did indeed, it seems, keep his part of the bargain. I was sent to a very prestigious boarding school in Broadstairs, which suited me just fine as, by the time I was of school age, my mother had met someone else.

"Not having too many choices in the prospective husband department with a child in tow, she agreed to marry him so that I would at least have a father. However, as it turned out, he was not exactly her knight in shining armour and I was definitely not part of his game plan. We disliked each other right from the start, as, true to her word, my mother would never divulge my lineage, so to speak. As a result, he regarded me as a constant reminder of my mother's secret past. We were both glad to be rid of each other, and I went off to school without a second thought about anything, other than to enjoy myself."

All this time, Chris had been watching Mark carefully, trying to figure out the guy behind the facade. Tim had given her a quick glimpse of the truth, but Mark's version showed that quite a bit had been left out, particularly how deeply it had all affected him.

"I graduated from school a star pupil, having nothing else to occupy my mind, and your secret would have remained safe forever," Mark continued, "if it had not been for my mother's best friend, who apparently had also worked for the company, on the marketing team. I had come home for the summer, after finishing college – still none the wiser about my history – ready to start making my way in the world. My mother wanted to throw a party for me to celebrate my academic success. I wasn't keen at first, but as my stepfather wasn't happy about it either, I went along with it to spite him."

He paused to smile at the memory.

"As the evening progressed, Audrey became more and more talkative until eventually she let slip just enough information to arouse my interest and start me thinking. A few careless words from her that night and my whole life changed. I turned from just another angry young man into one with a purpose."

Daniel started to reach out a hand to Mark, but thought better of it and returned his gaze to his glass.

"I never wanted anyone, other than Sally and I, to get hurt," Daniel said quietly. "That was unavoidable. But my father assured me that everything was being done to make sure you were happy. I thought about you a great deal over the years, but Caroline and I patched up our differences. She forgave me, believing that she was probably partly to blame. At least she was talking to me again. Simon was, of course, growing up and I had him to focus on, so I forced myself to believe that you were better off without me. I can see now that I may have been wrong."

"Oh, there's one more part of the story I should mention," Mark chimed in. "After my mother married she had another son. As it turned out, my stepfather was no better a father to him than he had been to me. Because I was away at school most of the time, I didn't see much of my half brother as he was growing up. However, as he grew older we spent more time together during the school and college holidays and discovered that we got on rather well, not least because of the shared resentment towards our father."

At this point, Mark looked towards Tim, who now had his turn to feel awkward at being the centre of attention.

"As Simon has already told you, this is Tim Myers, the company's receptionist," he said. "He is also my half brother."

"What," cried Simon. "Oh, great! What next... don't tell me, Christina is my long lost sister?"

He banged his empty glass down furiously on the table and threw himself back in the sofa, running his hand through his hair.

"Of course, not," exclaimed Chris indignantly. "I was just as much in the dark as you were until earlier this evening. Rest assured, I have several questions of my own that need answering."

She transferred her glare to Mark, who avoided it. Instead he turned his attention back to Daniel.

"After Audrey's revelations, curiosity kicked in and I started to imagine what it would be like to meet you," he declared. "When I suddenly found myself with access to all that money, I treated myself to a fast car in celebration and temporarily lost interest in you. When I finally became bored with the constant partying my curiosity returned and I resolved to make a concerted effort to find you.

"I knew the name of the company, but wasn't sure exactly where it was based. However, after a brief search on the Internet, I found its location. But I hadn't realised how widespread the organisation was and discovered that you had several offices around the world. As your son was listed as managing director, I made a reasonable assumption that you would be based in the London office, so I concentrated my efforts there."

He shot a nervous, sideways glance at Chris, who had her eyes covered, knowing that her part in the plot was about to be revealed.

"Tim was looking for a job, so when I read about a vacancy for a receptionist at Feldman & Son I suggested that he should apply," Mark continued. "He wasn't keen at first, but I managed to persuade him, as he had agreed to help me." He looked towards Tim. "Tim's been a great support to me, even though he hasn't always agreed with my methods. He put me up in his flat so that I could be close at hand and tried hard to keep me focussed. It couldn't have been easy for him and I don't want him to suffer for any of this. None of it was his fault."

He stared directly back at Daniel, shooting a brief glance at Simon first. Finally, lowering his head, he broached the subject of Chris.

"I hope Chris can forgive me for what I put her through too," he began slowly. "I didn't know that I was going to care for her as much as I do now."

He hesitated for a moment, before taking a deep breath and resuming.

"I was looking for a way to get information about you," he said to Daniel. "There was only so much Tim could find out, stuck in the reception area. But by the time he arrived at the job, you had retired through ill health. I thought it would look suspicious if Tim or I asked anyone for your address outright, so I decided that I needed to get to know someone on the inside."

Again he paused. This was proving harder than he thought, especially in front of everyone. He would have preferred to explain to Chris when they were alone. However, he was now committed.

"Tim told me that your son had employed a new assistant. He said her name was Christina, or Chris as everyone calls her, and that she worked closely with her boss. I didn't know how much she would know about you, but I thought she might be a good starting point. I engineered an accidental meeting with her one morning at a local sandwich bar she frequents, and eventually asked her out."

Chris bit her lip and felt her eyes moisten as the memory of that first meeting rushed back through her mind. Although she already knew from Tim that she had originally been a pawn in Mark's quest, she had desperately hoped that he had been exaggerating. However, as the truth fell from Mark's own lips, the reality of the situation struck home, like a dagger to her heart. How could she have been such a fool, she thought, as to believe that her luck with men was going to change? She allowed a tear to trickle its way down her face.

"The plan worked and we started seeing each other," continued

Mark. "I managed to find out a few snippets of information, but Chris is very loyal and gave nothing away that I didn't already know. I tried to stay as casual as possible and was careful not to say too much about myself, planning initially to walk away as soon as I had found out what I needed to know, covering my tracks in the process. But she turned out to be anything but the pushover I was expecting and started asking all sorts of questions that I didn't want to answer. I think deep down I always knew there was something different about Chris compared to the other girls I'd known. However, it wasn't until she finally walked out on me one night in the middle of a date that I realised I didn't just want her as a means to an end. I was actually beginning to care deeply about her."

He slid his hand towards Chris's, but she pulled it away and stared out through the window into the darkness.

Simon broke the tension by jumping up from the sofa.

"Alright, I've heard enough for one night," he snapped. "You'll forgive me if I don't throw my arms around you and say how great it is to have a new, unexpected baby brother. Welcome to the family and all that, but this is really doing my head in right now. I need time to take in what's gone on here tonight, and so too does my father I should think. I certainly believe you should all leave now before my mother returns. We can at least spare *her* any unnecessary shocks. I'll leave that to you, dad… you do it so well!"

With that, he swept out of the lounge and upstairs to his room, leaving the others in stunned silence.

CHAPTER 40

As the sound of Simon's bedroom door being slammed resounded through the house, the others sat for a while, unsure of who should make the first move.

It was Daniel who decided for them, reiterating Simon's suggestion that they should all leave now, before his wife returned. Simon was right, he did indeed have some explaining to do and it would be better if he did it when they were on their own.

The group individually said goodbye to him.

Last to leave was Mark, who hesitated at the lounge door and briefly cast a glance back at Daniel. Seeing that his father was lost in his own thoughts, he followed the others out.

Chris refused to accept a lift from Mark, barely able to look at him. Instead, she suggested to Tim that it would probably make sense to give their statements that evening, rather than driving all the way back to Esher the next day. He could drive her home afterwards, if he did not mind, she said. After giving Mark an apologetic look, Tim agreed. In truth, he was too tired to argue any more. Mark was left to drive home by himself and make his own arrangements with the police.

Alone, Daniel wandered into the kitchen. He pushed the chair, which Tim had used to secure Adrianna, back under the table. He replaced the tights in the washing basket and hung the tea towel back on the cupboard handle. Feeling the warmth of the oven, he remembered it was still on. Fortunately, he had not got round to putting the casserole in. He switched it off and looked at the saucepans full of vegetables on the hob, but the last thing he felt like doing was eat.

Locking the back door and switching off the kitchen light, he was walking back into the lounge as the front door opened and his wife appeared. She wiped her feet on the mat and took off her shoes.

She put on her slippers and smiled warmly at her husband.

"Hello dear," she said, giving him a peck on the cheek. "I think Devina is settled now. It was such a shock for her, but now she knows Jack is going to recover she can cope with the situation. How did it go this evening? What's Simon's new girlfriend like? Are they in the lounge? I'll just go and say hello."

Daniel took hold of both her hands and gently gazed into her questioning eyes.

"I need to tell you something, my dear, and you may need a stiff drink," he said calmly, leading her towards the lounge. "We've had quite an evening and I fear it's not over yet."

* * * * * *

Chris awoke on the Saturday morning to the sound of rain belting down on her bedroom window. As she opened her eyes, and the events of the previous night gradually began to seep back into her consciousness, she started to cry. She had been so worn out that she had fallen asleep as soon as her head hit the pillow, but now the full force of the revelations flooded back with a vengeance.

The thought of facing the day with nothing but her own painful recollections for company filled her with dread. So she sunk further under the duvet and lay listening to the rain. The day outside seemed as bleak as her life felt at that moment, and she was in no hurry to greet it.

Eventually, all cried out, she got up and went into the bathroom. She studied her face in the mirror. Her eyes were red and puffy and she found herself wondering who was staring back at her. It definitely was not the girl who she saw reflected two days previously. How quickly so much could change in just one day, she thought sadly as she got into the shower and let the water wash soothingly over her.

Chris hardly left the sofa for the rest of the day. She listened repeatedly to Sade, reliving the last night she and Mark had spent together in her flat. It seemed like months ago rather than three days and the more she thought about his warm embrace and soft, sensual kisses, the more upset she became. Part of her hated him for his deception, but she kept remembering the last words he said to her outside Daniel Feldman's house – that he loved her. She had replied that she needed time and space to think, and that she did not want to speak to him until she had done that. How could she trust anything he said to her? Having been found out, was he not simply trying to extricate himself from his tangled web of deceit? But then, if he did not care about her, surely he would simply walk away, unconcerned about what she thought of him.

In truth, she did not know what to believe and, by the end of the day, she was still none the wiser.

Chris was still wrestling with her thoughts and feelings on Sunday, trying to come to terms with all that had gone before. She had not left the flat all weekend, but she was totally exhausted and emotionally drained. She was tired of her own company and preparing to go to bed early, when the telephone rang. Afraid that it would be Mark, and not feeling ready to speak to him, she let the answerphone take the call.

Hearing Tessa's voice, she grabbed the receiver and stopped her mid-message.

"Hi Tess," she exclaimed, a feeling of warmth rising in her at the sound of her friend's voice. "Sorry, but I wasn't sure who was ringing. I thought it might be Mark, or worse… my mother."

Tessa sighed audibly.

"What's he done now?" she asked patiently. "I thought you guys had sorted things out. I can't keep up with your love life these days. Sometimes I long for the old Chris and her aversion to dating."

She started laughing, but stopped as she realised that Chris had begun to cry.

"Oh, sweetie," she cried. "What's the matter? What's happened? Have you and Mark had a fight? I'm sure you'll sort it out soon. Please don't cry."

Not knowing quite what to do, but wanting to be there to comfort her friend, Tessa continued to ramble on, searching for the right words.

"Oh Tess," Chris sobbed. "It's all such a mess and I don't know what to think or do. So much happened Friday that I don't know where to start. I'm so confused. I really need a shoulder to cry on, and yours is the only shoulder I feel comfortable with."

Tessa suggested they meet up the next evening at Toppers.

"Light some scented candles, have a hot bath and get a good night's sleep," she advised gently. "Tomorrow you can get it all off your chest. Remember what I always say. There's no problem that can't be solved by a bottle or two of good wine. I should know."

CHAPTER 41

Chris had slept so deeply after her traumatic weekend that the alarm clock had trouble rousing her when it went off on Monday morning. It was going to be an awkward day, she thought, assuming that Simon was going to come into the office at all. She allowed herself a few minutes to assemble her thoughts, trying to rehearse what she was going to say to him – whether to mention Friday's drama or act as if nothing had happened. Leaping out of bed and heading for the bathroom, she concluded that the best thing would be to play it by ear.

The weather had definitely taken a turn for the worse, and as she stepped outside to make her way to the tube a gust of cold wind made her pull her coat tightly around her.

The tube was even more packed than usual. The children would be going back to school soon and it looked as if most people had returned from their holidays and re-joined the morning rush hour. She was not looking forward to the winter, with its long, dark nights and lonely evenings huddled in front of the television with a ready-meal. She rarely ventured far on cold winter nights.

Tim was sitting at the reception desk, drinking a cup of coffee. She wondered why she was surprised to see him. After all, he still worked for the company – as far as she knew. Perhaps, now that everything was out in the open and his part in it over, she had expected him to disappear. Oddly, she found herself comforted by the sight of him. During their journeys to and from Daniel Feldman's house last week they had got to know each other better and she realised he was merely a fellow victim of Mark's plots and schemes.

"Morning Tim," she said, smiling apprehensively at him, unsure what his reaction was going to be. She was relieved when he beamed back at her.

"Morning Chris," he replied cheerfully. "How are you feeling after our adventure on Friday? I haven't seen boss man yet, so I'm hoping I've still got a job by the end of the day."

He gave a half laugh, but Chris could tell that he was trying to hide his concern. Despite everything, she felt it would be simply wrong if Simon fired Tim just because he had wanted to help his brother.

"He shouldn't take it out on you, just because his family keep secrets from each other," she said, trying to reassure him. "It's his father he should be venting his anger on. Daniel Feldman has a lot to answer for, although people in his position always seem to come out on top."

She gave him another supportive smile and then made her way to the lifts.

When Chris reached her office, as Tim had suggested, Simon was not in his. So she made herself a coffee and settled down to check her diary and start making some calls. Things were going well with her new clients and Colin Matthews from Taylor-Wood had recommended her to a friend. Her career, at least, was showing signs of progress. Pity her love life was not as successful, she thought, as she picked up the phone to check progress with Antonio in Rome.

Simon was missing all morning, but, just after lunch, Chris saw him walk past as he entered his office, shutting the door behind him without saying a word. She saw him, through the glass partition, mouthing a thank you to Mrs Summers for the coffee she brought into him and then he sat in silence. He seemed to be staring aimlessly at his computer, so Chris assumed he was checking his emails and went back to concentrating on her own work.

Hearing nothing from him for over an hour, the suspense got the better of her. Getting up from her desk, she walked towards his office and tapped on the door. She received no response, so tapped again. This time a quiet voice invited her to come in.

"I just thought I'd ask how you are," she began cautiously. "I was worried about you all weekend. Is there anything I can do?"

Simon continued to stare at his screen, where the login box was still requesting his password. It was almost as if he was unaware of her presence, or indeed anything else in the room. When he looked up at her, his usual kind face was white with sleep deprivation. He looked deeply unhappy and Chris at once felt an affinity with him – after all, they had both been innocent victims caught up in the secret pasts of other people.

"My mother was devastated by your boyfriend's appearance in her life," he said. "It brought my father's betrayal cruelly back to her, as if it had only happened yesterday. She made him sleep in the spare room and wouldn't speak to him all day Saturday. She was a little calmer by the time I left on Sunday, but I'm not sure how things are going to be between them in the future. Only they can work that one out. Funny though, after the initial shock, she seemed to accept Mark turning up, as if she had always expected it one day.

"But what really hurt her was learning of dad's callous treatment of his old friend, Roberto. She got to know the family quite well after marrying my father, but, because he kept making excuses not to visit Monteriggioni, she lost touch. She had no idea what became of them, much less that dad had been indirectly to blame for Roberto's tragic death. She now realises only too well why dad had been so reluctant to return there."

Chris walked around his desk and put her hand on his shoulder. Simon tensed up, but then relaxed into her grip. He raised his hand and put it over hers. Chris realised that she had to do something to help him get his life back on track. He was a good man and did not deserve to be torn apart in this way. He had done nothing but support her since she started working for him and now it was her turn to reciprocate.

"I'm sorry about Adrianna," she said hesitantly. "I know how deeply you felt about her. If it's any consolation – and it probably isn't right now – I feel betrayed too. I think we have both paid dearly for wearing our hearts on our sleeves."

Simon looked up at her and gave her a sympathetic smile, patting her hand as he did so.

"Looks like it," he replied. "Although, as much as it pains me to say it, I don't think Mark was being as deceitful as Adrianna. Now that I've had time to think things through, after he realised he liked you, I really think he was trying to protect you from what he felt he had to do. Don't be too hard on him for my sake. I think life's dealt him enough knocks. Money isn't everything you know. I should know. I spent enough of my youth being pampered to compensate for my father not being around. I understand that, to a young boy, money is ultimately no substitute for the love and friendship of a father."

He returned his gaze to his computer screen and, releasing Chris's hand, typed in his password. The screen danced into life revealing his email list.

"OK," he declared, pulling himself together. "Back to work. I think I've spent enough time wallowing in my own self-pity. One of us Feldmans has got to show a bit of backbone."

Chris made to return to her office, but as she reached the door, she remembered her date with Tessa that night at the wine bar. Although she originally wanted a heart-to-heart with her friend, she felt so sorry for Simon that she found herself inviting him along.

"I know you probably don't like to mix socially with your staff," she said, turning to look at him, "but I'm drowning my sorrows with my friend Tessa – and a good bottle of wine or two – across the road tonight. You should join us. I think we could both do with a relaxing evening among friends, don't you?"

Simon hesitated for a moment, and was about to decline her offer, but before the words had left his lips he changed his mind.

"Damn it," he cried, banging the desk with both hands. "I think you're right. Why not? If only to show that at least one member of my uptight family is normal. What time are you seeing your friend?"

Chris laughed and promised to knock on his door when she was leaving so they could walk across to Toppers together.

She left the room and went back to her own office, grinning to herself. Today had turned out to be better than expected.

CHAPTER 42

Toppers was packed when they arrived, but Chris spotted Tessa at a table by the window and guided Simon towards her. Tessa was surprised to see Chris with someone and, not realising he was her boss, raised her eyebrows and gave Chris a knowing glance.

"Hi, sweetie," she chirped, throwing her arms around Chris and pecking her on the check. She held out her hand to Simon. "I'm Tessa. Chris didn't tell me she was bringing such a good-looking friend with her. You dark horse, Chris."

Chris took off her coat, laying it over the back of the chair nearest to her.

"For heaven's sake, Tess," she laughed, slightly embarrassed on Simon's behalf. "What are you like? This is Simon Feldman, my boss. We both need cheering up tonight, so put your eyes back in their sockets and start working your magic."

Tessa apologised profusely to Simon, and while she was busy trying to hide her embarrassment, Simon pulled up a chair for Chris to sit down. This action was not lost on Tessa and she made a mental note that he was definitely going to be worthy of her attention tonight.

Simon scrutinised the wine list. He seemed quite impressed with the selection.

"What would you like to drink, ladies?" he asked. "My treat. Red or white?"

"We usually drink white," Chris replied, glancing at Tessa. "But red might make a nice change, if that's OK with you?"

"Fine with me," he agreed. "They have a bottle of the Chianti we had in Rome, Christina. Why don't we go for that? It was a great evening." He hesitated, remembering what else had happened that night. "Before it took a turn for the worse, that is," he frowned. "Still, no point in dwelling on what might have been is there. I'll go and order a couple of bottles. I think that should start the ball rolling."

He got up to make his way to the bar, leaving Tessa and Chris to catch up.

"Wow, what a hot guy," said Tessa excitedly, eyeing Simon up and down as he strolled towards the bar. "You certainly kept him quiet!"

Chris rolled her eyes, realising what was going through Tessa's mind.

"Careful Tess," Chris cautioned her. "You've both recently had a rough ride emotionally. If you're planning on making a move on him, treat him gently and keep it light. He has a few wounds to heal."

"I'm sure I can help to heal them," Tessa said reassuringly. "I can do sensitive, when the occasion demands."

She winked at Chris, who shook her head in mock disbelief. Tessa was incorrigible, she thought.

More people had entered the wine bar and Simon was caught up in a throng of people vying for the barman's attention. Chris and Tessa lost sight of him altogether and as Chris scanned the bar for her boss, she was unaware someone else had approached her. He stood quietly by the side of the table, waiting for her to notice him.

Giving up on her search for Simon, Chris returned her attention to Tessa. Realising that Tessa was looking past her at something, she turned around to find out what it was.

"Hi Chris," said Mark quietly, running a nervous finger along the table top and smiling warily at her, cautiously trying to gauge her reaction. "I know you wanted time to think, but the weekend has been hell without hearing your voice or sharing your thoughts. When this morning came and you still hadn't rung me, I was afraid that I'd never see you again."

Tessa decided that it would be prudent to give them some privacy.

"I think I'll just go and give Simon a hand at the bar," she said, getting up and leaving the two of them silently sizing each other up.

Chris looked at Mark for a while, saying nothing. She had been so angry with him when she left him bewildered on Daniel's driveway, but now that he was standing in front of her, like a lost schoolboy, her heart started to melt. She had an overwhelming urge to throw her arms around his neck. However, he *had* caused her to wallow in misery all weekend. He did not deserve to get away with that so easily, so she maintained a poker face.

"What do you want me to say Mark?" she snapped. "Have you any idea how hurtful it was to find out that I was little more than a means to an end? And if your feelings for me really did change, why couldn't you have told me who you really were and what you were planning to do?"

She held his gaze and could see that he was squirming. Uncharacteristically, she felt a rush of power. She was not going to let him off the hook easily, now that she felt in control of her emotions.

"Didn't you trust me?" she continued. "Did you think I would go running to Simon and spoil your… reunion? Or did you think so little of me that my feelings didn't even register on your radar?"

Mark's head had sunk towards his chest while this tirade was hurled at him. He knew he deserved every harsh word she could throw at him, and had resolved to accept any verbal tongue-lashing she decided was necessary. He just wanted her to forgive him.

He pulled a chair out from under the table and sat down beside her, picking up her hand and holding it between his own.

"Chris," he begged. "I've been such an idiot. I was so self-obsessed with getting what I wanted that I didn't think about the effect I was having on others… especially you. I didn't realise that in meeting you I had, for the first time in my life, found someone I actually wanted to be with. By the time it did eventually dawn on me, things had become way too complicated. I didn't want to risk losing you before I had managed to resolve my issues – one way or the other. I honestly didn't think it was fair to drag you into something that wasn't your problem. I am so sorry. Please say you'll forgive me. I couldn't bear for you to hate me."

Chris sighed. It was no good, she really was useless at being hard-nosed, and she soon realised there was no way, with those penetrating blue eyes gazing imploringly into hers, that she was going to keep this charade up for much longer. Surrendering to her feelings, she gave Mark a resigned smile, leant towards him and gently kissed his lips.

"I forgive you," she relented. "But don't think that means I'm a pushover, Mark Dempster. Do something like that to me again and you'll wish that Giovanni *had* shot you."

She scowled at him menacingly, before dissolving into laughter. Mark felt the relief flood through him as he squeezed her hand more tightly than ever.

"I never got the chance to thank you for saving me," he said, shifting one of his hands to stroke her cheek. "Remind me not to get into an argument with you while there are flower pots around. You're pretty handy."

Tessa and Simon arrived back at the table. Simon was carrying two bottles of Chianti and Tessa had the glasses. As Mark and Simon made eye contact, Chris felt a moment of panic. She had forgotten that Simon was there and was fearful as to what his reaction would be. She took a deep breath and waited for the storm to break. Tessa, completely in the dark about Friday night, felt the tension too and sat down, shooting Chris a questioning look.

After what seemed like an eternity, Simon raised his eyebrows and his expression became relaxed.

"Well, brother," he said, putting the bottles down on the table. "Looks like I can't escape you now, as you appear to be the object of my assistant's desire. I feel I have to warn you, though. She's now a ruthless businesswoman – so don't mess with her. Oh, and by the way," he added, sitting down. "Joining the Feldman family won't be a picnic either. We're all completely screwed up you know, so good luck."

He raised his hand to a passing waiter, requesting another glass. The waiter scuttled away and by the time he returned, Simon had poured wine into the other three glasses. He filled the fourth, handed the glasses around and proposed a toast.

"Here's to truth and revenge," he declared. "The quest for them nearly destroyed us, but now let's hope that finding one and outriding the other has freed us to get on with our lives."

The others echoed the toast, poor Tessa none the wiser as to the meaning, but joining in all the same.

As the evening progressed, Simon steadily became more relaxed. He and Tessa really hit it off. Chris watched them laughing and chatting, so naturally at ease in each other's company, and she knew that Simon was going to be alright. Tessa was exactly what he needed in his life right now and she felt pleased to have been instrumental in bringing them together.

As for her and Mark, they needed to get to know each other all over again. This time though, at least she knew what and who she was dealing with. She watched him carefully as he shared his plans with her, memorising every detail of his face. For the last few weeks she had felt totally at sea. Every time she had thought herself settled, a wave of confusion had knocked her off course. Now, at last, she felt she had reached a safe harbour.

Mark stopped talking, put his arm around her and, pulling her to him, whispered in her ear.

"How about we let those two have some alone time? We could go back to your flat and start again where we left off. You, me… oh, and Sade," he joked.

Chris dug him in the ribs, but was only too pleased to agree.

Standing up, she retrieved her coat and bag and turned to say goodbye to Tessa and Simon. They were totally engrossed in each other – Simon now had his arm around Tessa and was whispering into her ear. Chris leant towards them and waved to attract their attention, to let them know she and Mark were leaving. They fleetingly acknowledged her, waving back, before resuming their besotted positions. Chris broke into a broad grin as she and Mark made their way past the other drinkers to the door.

The wind gathered pace again, and Chris automatically wrapped her coat tightly around her to keep out the cold. Seeing her shiver, Mark pulled her closer to him. He kissed her long and seductively and she felt the warmth from his body begin to radiate through her.

He gazed into her eyes seriously.

"I love you, Christina Newman," he whispered. "You're the best thing that's happened to me in my mixed up life, and I don't intend to risk losing you ever again. That's a promise."

He hailed a taxi as it came around the corner, deciding it would be wise to retrieve his car later. He was not in a hurry to speak to any more policemen.

"After you," he chuckled, opening the taxi door and bowing to Chris. "We mustn't keep Sade waiting."

Chris giggled and playfully slapped his arm before climbing into the back of the cab. Mark jumped in after her, slamming the taxi door behind him and calling out Chris's address to the driver.

Snuggled beside him, Chris no longer felt cold, just a warm glow of contentment. She had no idea what the future held, but right now it did not matter.

ABOUT THE AUTHOR

Sheila Rawlings was educated at Bexley Technical High School for Girls and went on to complete a 4-year course in Graphic Design at Medway College of Art and Design in Chatham, Kent.

After graduating from college, she worked as a graphic designer for two mail order companies, designing and producing their catalogues. She then worked for several years as a graphic designer and production manager for a magazine publisher, producing a weekly trade journal, as well as various other publications. During that time she also assisted their PR and marketing department, designing exhibition stands for various clients.

Working with journalists, and therefore the written word, she rekindled her love of storytelling, which prompted her to write this novel.